Dusty Rhodes
P. O. Box 7
Greenwood, AR 72936

THE TOWN TAMER

"The Life and Times of J. C. Holderfield"

A Western Novel

By

Dusty Rhodes

"THE TOWN TAMER"

The life and times of J. C. Holderfield

Cover art by Page Holland
Cover design by Julie Sartain

Published by Dusty Rhodes Books in USA
The characters and events in this book are fictional.
Any resemblance to persons either living or dead is
strictly coincidental.

ISBN 978-1-4507-4710-3

"THE TOWN TAMER"

By

Dusty Rhodes

CHAPTER I

"Two life changing events shaped my life and are forever lodged in my memory.
The first was the day my pa was killed in a tragic accident when a tree fell on him.

The second was eight months later when my ma died and
I was left completely alone—I was thirteen years old."
~ J. C. Holderfield~

John Claude and Edna Holderfield had a son born on
January 2, 1832. His mother decided to name their son
after his father and used his father's initials—J. C.

When he was six years old, his ma put a salt pork
biscuit in a lard can dinner bucket and sent J. C. down the
dusty road to the one-room schoolhouse in Pikesville,
Tennessee—it was six miles.

Every weekday for three years, he walked six miles
to school and then walked back home after school
dismissed. On those rare days when it was too wet to
plow or work in the field and Pa didn't need their mule
for something else, he was allowed to ride Ole Tom, their
big, brown Missouri mule, to school.

When he turned nine years old, his pa told him he
had enough schooling and it was time to go to work.
"You're a big, strong boy. Much bigger than most boys
your age," his pa told him. "It's time you started helping
with the farm work."

From that day until his pa's death, they worked side-
by-side.

"Get up, son!" were the words that jarred young J. C.
from sleep most every morning of his young life. "It's
almost daylight and we've got a lot of work to do today!"
Goodness knows it took a lot of work to scratch a living
out of forty acres of hill-country land on the backside of
Walden Ridge near Pikesville, Tennessee.

Every day was the same. Before breakfast, J. C. did
his chores. That consisted of milking their jersey cow,
slopping their hog, and feeding the chickens. After

breakfast, his ma packed what little leftovers there were into a lard bucket for his and Pa's lunch. Lunch usually consisted of two sausage or salt pork biscuits and a fruit jar of milk, but it shore tasted good after a hard morning's work.

In early spring, they plowed and planted every inch of their forty acres. After the crop was planted, his job was to keep the weeds and johnson grass chopped out of the forty-acre crop.

Harvest time was always a busy time. J. C. and his pa worked from daylight until dark, six days a week. Come Sunday, their family hitched Ole Tom to their farm wagon and drove into Pikesville to church.

J. C. always looked forward to Sunday, because he got to see Carolyn Glover at church. Her father was a hard man. He owned the mercantile store in Pikesville and didn't allow his daughter to talk to boys—especially J. C.—but he liked looking at her anyway.

After the crops were in, it was time to start chopping down trees and cutting wood for winter—that's how John Claude Holderfield met his death.

J. C. was trimming limbs from a felled tree, getting it ready to drag to the house where they would chop it up for firewood. His pa was chopping down a big oak tree nearby.

J. C. didn't actually see what happened, but he heard his pa holler. He twisted a frightened look in time to see the big oak knock his pa to the ground.

He raced the short distance to find his pa pinned underneath the heavy trunk of the oak tree—he wasn't moving.

"Pa! Pa!" he screamed, but his screams were only met with silence.

He looked around frantically to find something—anything—to pry the tree off his pa. His first thought was to run for help—but where? His ma couldn't help! And it was six miles to town! Besides, there wasn't time! He had to get the tree off his pa!

He did the only thing he knew to do—he grabbed the ax his pa had been using and set to work, frantically chopping the large trunk of the tree in two so he could get his pa out from under it.

By the time his ax broke through the trunk and he was able to tug his pa free, he knew it was too late. He dropped the ax and ran all the way to the house.

He quickly hitched the mule to the wagon. J. C. and his mother drove to the woods to bring his pa's body back to the house.

They buried John Claude Holderfield on the little hill behind their slat-board cabin. Besides J. C. and his ma, the only others to attend the funeral was their closest neighbors, Mr. and Mrs. Venable.

After her husband's death, Edna Holderfield just seemed to lose her desire to go on living. She sat for hours, staring into space at nothing. She barely spoke.

J. C. tried his best to carry on. He did the chores: chopped the wood, built the fire every morning, carried in water, cooked what little they had to eat, and worked until well after dark every day, but there was just no way for a thirteen-year-old boy to do everything that had to be done. Mr. and Mrs. Venable came and helped J. C. kill and butcher their only hog. Mr. Venable showed J. C. how to smoke the meat and cure it so it would keep. Between the hog meat, a fried chicken now and then, and the squirrels and rabbits he was able to kill with his pa's old Kentucky, muzzle-loading, long rifle, they managed to make it through the winter.

Four months after his pa's death, J. C. hitched Ole Tom to the plow and set in plowing the fields, getting ready for spring planting. It was back-breaking work for a grown man, let alone a thirteen-year-old boy.

He worked from daylight until dark. Finally, the plowing was done and it was time for planting. He knew his pa always ran a bill at Glover's Mercantile in Pikesville. He had gone with his pa several times and knew that's where they got their seeds for planting.

He told his ma where he was going, hitched Ole Tom to the wagon, and headed into town.

"Mornin', Mr. Glover, sir," he said, walking up to the store owner.

The store owner twisted a scowling look at him. "Oh, it's you—the Holderfield boy. Heard about your pa's accident—too bad. How's your ma?"

"She's been feeling poorly since Pa died. I come in to get the seeds for planting our spring crop and a sack of flour for Ma."

"Well, fact is, we've got a problem, boy. I been meaning to talk to your ma at church, but ain't seen her since your pa died. Tell your ma she needs to come in and talk to me. We've got some serious business we need to discuss."

J. C. didn't understand what the store owner was saying.

"I—I don't know if she can do that, sir. Like I said, she's been feeling poorly since Pa died. She don't get out hardly a'tall."

"I see. Well, I'm afraid I can't advance your ma any more credit until she settles up what I'm owed. Your pa always come in and settled up his bill after his crop was in, but last year, he never come. I suppose I'll have to ride out and have a talk with her and settle some things."

"But, Mr. Glover, sir, we need that sack of flour mighty bad; we're slap-dab out and I need the seed to get my crop planted. Can't I get the seed and flour and you can talk to Ma later?"

"'Fraid not, boy. Your ma needs to settle up last year's bill before I can let you have anything else. She owes me fifty-seven dollars and twenty-two cents."

J. C. didn't know what to do. He nodded understanding, even if he didn't. He turned and left the store without another word, got back in the wagon, and drove home—totally dejected.

He tried to explain to his ma what Mr. Glover had said, but wasn't sure she understood or even heard him. She just stared at him with a blank expression and didn't say anything.

It was hard getting by without flour, but he made do. He used the last of their ground cornmeal, added some water, and made fried flap-jacks. That, and salt pork was their usual meal.

Time was getting by. The days were warming up. Green shoots of grass were sticking through the ground. He knew he ought to be planting his crop, but without seed, how could he? He didn't know what to do.

Four weeks passed. Finally, on a warm Sunday afternoon, Mr. Glover and a big, hard-looking man with a badge pinned on his shirt-front drove up in a buggy. J. C. saw them and went out on the front porch to see what they wanted.

"*Howdy*, boy," Mr. Glover said. "Is your ma home? We need to see her."

"She's here," J. C. said. He turned and stepped back inside.

His ma was sitting in her usual place—the rocking chair beside the pot-bellied wood stove in the front room.

"Ma, Mr. Glover and some fellow with a law badge are outside. They want to talk to you."

She didn't move or act like she heard him.

"Ma! Did you hear what I said? Mr. Glover from the store is outside. He's got the law with him. He wants to talk to you!"

She still didn't move or act like she even heard what he said. Frustrated, he turned and went back to the front door.

"She ain't feeling good. Can you come back later?"

Mr. Glover's face flushed beet-red. He climbed quickly from the buggy with a real mad on and headed toward the front door, followed closely by the big lawman.

"No! We can't come back later! We need to talk to her right now!"

They shoved past J. C. and stomped into the front room.

"Mrs. Holderfield, I told your son I need to talk with you about your bill at the store. I know you're having a hard time since your husband passed on, but times are hard for everybody!

"John Claude owes me fifty-seven dollars and twenty-two cents from last year. He put up your house and land for collateral. You need to make some kind of arrangements to pay me, or I'm afraid I'll have to call your note.

"I don't want to have to do it, but if I'm forced to, I will. That means I'll have to foreclose on your house and land. If that happens, you'll have to vacate this place and turn it over to me.

"Everybody hereabouts knows I'm a reasonable man. I'll give you another two months, but if I'm not paid by then, I'll file papers to evict you and the boy."

They turned and left, climbed into their buggy, and drove away. J. C. heard what Mr. Glover said, but didn't really understand what all of it meant.

We brought in our crop last year, just like always. Hadn't Pa paid his bill at the store before he died? If not, what happened to the money? How can they just take our house and land? What will we do? Where will we live?

He tried to question his ma about where Pa hid his money, but she seemed to be withdrawing deeper and deeper into her shell. She never bothered to cook any more; J. C. did everything now. All his mother did was sit in her rocker and stare off into space.

He searched every inch of the house, trying to find the money his father got for last year's crop, but could find nothing. He dug around the yard in every place he thought the money might be buried, but still found nothing.

He searched the small shed they used for a barn—still nothing. He was at his wits' end.

A week turned into a month, and then two. His ma now stayed in bed all time. He waited on her, hand and foot. He fed her when she would try to eat, which wasn't often. He could tell she was getting frail and weak.

Mrs. Venable made the long trip every now and then to check on his mother. Each time, she brought some vittles for them to eat, usually boiled turnips, greens, and a pone of cornbread. He made up his mind to pay her back for her kindness someday.

J. C. saw the lawman coming in his buggy and walked out on the front porch as he drove up.

"I need to see your ma, son," the big lawman said, withdrawing some folded papers from his suit coat pocket.

"She's sick in bed, sir. She don't know nobody, no how."

"I still need to see her," he said, climbing from his buggy.

J. C. showed him the small bedroom where his ma was. She lay there with her eyes closed.

"Mrs. Holderfield, can you hear me? This is Sheriff Mort Stallings. The two months Mr. Glover gave you is up. I'm here to serve eviction papers. This order from the judge says you and the boy have got to vacate the property within seven days. The property has been awarded to Henry Glover for non-payment of debt. I'm sorry, Mrs. Holderfield, but the law's the law."

With that said, he laid the papers on the bed beside J. C's ma, turned, and left.

Silent tears escaped J. C.'s eyes. He felt helpless, frightened, alone, desperate.

What am I gonna do? Why are they taking our home? Where are we gonna go? Ma's sick in bed! How can I take care of her?

J. C. ran from the house and around behind the small shed and sat down with his back against the weathered wall—and cried. For the first time in his memory—he cried.

Three days later—his ma died. He walked into the bedroom that morning to try to feed her some rabbit soup. She looked unusually white and still. He shook her, but she didn't respond. He touched her wrinkled face—it was cold. That's when he knew she was gone.

Mr. Venable helped J. C. dig a grave beside his pa and buried his mother there the next day. The only ones there were him and Mr. and Mrs. Venable.

"What you got in mind to do, son?" Mr. Venable asked after the grave was filled in.

"Don't know, Mr. Venable, sir. I've thought on it until my head hurts. I just don't know what to do," he answered honestly.

"We talked about asking you to come live with us. We'd like to take you in, son, but we're barely making it as it is without another mouth to feed. You understand?"

J. C. nodded his head.

"You and Mrs. Venable have done more'n anybody else around here. I'll get by."

With tears in his eyes and a huge knot in his stomach, he watched them as they drove away. He had never felt so lonely in his whole, short life.

For a long time he sat on the steps of the front porch, trying to figure out what to do. The lawman said he would be back to throw them off their place. Now, he was the only one that needed throwing.

Darkness surrounded him and he was still sitting there. Somewhere a whippoorwill called, but J. C. hardly heard it.

Ole Tom stood nearby, tied to a fence post near the shed. Two tow sacks were tied across his bare back. Beside the big mule, also tied with a rope halter, Bessie, their Jersey milk cow, stood patiently, swishing flies with her long tail.

J. C. stood nearby, barefooted, and wearing his best patched bib overalls and work shirt, with the butt of his pa's long barrel rifle resting against the ground and held with one hand.

Tears trailed across his cheeks as he watched the orange flames eat their way up the side of their house. Like a hungry monster, they leaped higher and higher into the darkening sky, consuming the only home J. C. had ever known.

If I can't have it—nobody will! he thought.

His throat was full and his heart was empty. His stomach ached with fright.

Turning, he untied Ole Tom's reins and the short rope that held Bessie, before swinging his leg over the mule's back and riding away.

CHAPTER II

The night was half spent when J. C. rode within sight of the Venable's place. The house was dark. While still a good ways off, he reined to a stop and slid from his mule. He tied Ole Tom to a low-hanging limb and quietly led the Jersey milk cow toward the house.

At the yard, he tied Bessie to a fence post. He paused for a long minute and stared at the cow he had cared for and loved for most of his life. His hand brushed lovingly along her neck. The cow looked at him with her big, dark, sad-looking eyes as if she knew what was happening. He patted her and walked away—the cow was all he had to give for the kindness the Venables had shown him and his ma.

He untied his mule, swung onto his back, and pointed his nose west.

He crossed the Sequatchie River just south of Pikesville before daylight. He had no idea where he was headed. All he knew was he wanted to be a long ways away before they discovered he had burned the house.

By mid-morning, he was in the foothills of the mountains. He had heard talk about the Cumberland Plateau and supposed that might be the name of the mountains he was riding through.

Just before good dark, he came to another river. He had no idea what it was called, but he camped beside it that night. He built a small fire, ate a bite from what little salt pork he had left in his tow sack, covered himself with the single blanket he had brought, and went to sleep beside the fire.

In the darkness of pre-dawn and in his half-asleep awareness, he waited, anticipating his pa's authoritative voice ordering him to *get up*—but the order never came.

He blinked himself awake and suddenly realized where he was. As he thought about the events that brought him to this time, fear surged through him. Even though he knew he would be in trouble with the law, he didn't regret burning the house.

Mr. Glover will be madder than an old setting hen, he figured. *He'll send that big lawman after me. If they catch me, I'll most likely spend the rest of my life in jail. Well, he's shore 'nuff got it to do. I'm gonna get myself as far away from Pikesville as Ole Tom can carry me.*

With that thought settled in his mind, he quickly rose and scooped up handfuls of dirt and covered the few remaining live coals from last night's fire. He watered Ole Tom, picked up his pa's Kentucky long rifle, and swung a leg over his mule's bare back and pointed his nose toward the west.

He wasn't in any particular hurry since he had no idea where he was going. He meandered along, keeping

Ole Tom's pace slow, allowing his mule to snatch a mouthful of grass as he plodded along.

Along about late afternoon of his second day on the trail, he came upon a road going the same direction he was headed and decided to follow it for a spell.

Up ahead, he saw two fellows on horses riding his direction. As they drew nearer, he could see they were hard-looking men. They both carried long rifles similar to his. Their's lay cross-wise across their saddles. The skinny horses they rode looked gaunt and half-starved. Their ribs showed clearly through tight-stretched skin. Their saddles were as used-up as their horses. The men eyed him with hard stares as they approached.

When they met on the road, both men reined their horses to a stop.

They were dirty looking. Their clothes were might near as ragged and used up as his. Both had heavy, tobacco-stained beards. Both wore leather scabbards with large hunting knives in them.

J. C. judged both men to be about his pa's age.

"Hold up there, boy!" one of them said gruffly.

J. C. tried to ride past them without replying, but one of them wheeled his horse and grabbed Ole Tom's reins.

"I said, *hold up!* You deaf or something?" the man shouted angrily. "That's a mighty big rifle you got there. Where'd a boy like you get a gun like that? You stole it, didn't you? Let me see it!"

"Didn't steal it," J. C. protested in a shaky voice. "It's my pa's,"

"I said, *let me see it!*" the man shouted even louder, leaning over and snatching it out of J. C.'s hand. The man looked the rifle over carefully.

"You got any money, boy?" the man asked, turning his attention away from the rifle and back to J. C.

"Come on, Clem," the other fellow said. "You can tell by looking at him he ain't got no more money than we do. Let him alone and let's go."

"Shut your trap!" the first man shouted. "I'm talking to this here boy, not you! I asked if you had any money?"

"I ain't," J. C. said quietly. "Can I have my rifle back now?"

"I took a liking to this here rifle. Decided I'm gonna keep it."

"But it's my pa's!"

"Not any more. It's mine now," he said, releasing Ole Tom's reins and reining his horse around.

J. C. sat atop his mule and watched helplessly as they rode away. He heard the one that stole his rifle laughing as they rode out of sight.

Their campsite was a good one. They had chosen a small clearing surrounded by a thick grove of scrub cedar. A small creek lay only a few yards away. Their two horses were hobbled nearby and grazed lazily on plentiful, green grass.

J. C. had left his mule tied in a thicket several hundred yards downstream and now lay behind a bunch of waist-high bushes no more than forty yards from the men's camp. He watched as they passed a jug of moonshine back and forth between themselves.

From their slurred words and loud laughter, he judged they would soon pass out in a drunken stupor; at least that was what he was hoping—he waited.

Luckily, there was only a thin slice of moon that ducked in and out from behind thick, low-lying clouds in a pitch-black sky.

While he waited, he planned. His searching gaze chose both his approach and his escape route. He had no weapon. Likely a weapon would be worthless against two armed, grown men anyway. If he was discovered, his only hope for escape was his speed—he knew he could outrun them if he had to.

He didn't have long to wait. The drunken conversation between the two men soon died away to silence—still he waited longer.

He was nervous and scared. Sweat slickened the palms of his hands, but the anger he felt inside overpowered all other emotions. They had stolen his rifle—he had to have it to survive—he meant to get it back or die trying.

He had spent some time in the woods and had learned the art of stalking all kind of wildlife. As he cautiously left his hiding place, he pretended he was approaching a deer. He moved slowly, cautiously placing each hand to avoid anything that would make a sound and alert his enemy. He inched forward on his hands and knees.

As he drew nearer, he could hear both robbers snoring loudly. The campfire had burned down to a pile of glowing embers.

In the dim light, he could barely make out the vague forms of the sleeping robbers. He inched forward. One of the men was now within an arm's reach.

J. C. saw two rifles lying near the closest man and knew that one of them was his. Beside the rifles was a leather scabbard holding the bone-handled hunting knife he had seen earlier. He took them all.

Crawfishing backward, he retreated to the edge of the camp and left his stolen things in a pile. He then returned to the other sleeping man and took his rifle also.

He quickly hurried downstream a ways, tossed the extra rifles into the creek, and returned again to the camp. He unhobbled the horses, took up the reins, and led them quietly away.

He paused long enough to recover his rifle and the knife he had stolen, and then led the two horses downstream to where he had left his mule. He mounted, and leading the stolen horses, rode away.

He led the two robbers' horses until mid-afternoon of the next day before turning them loose. He figured by the time the robbers found their horses, he would be too far away for them to trail.

When he stopped for the night after the fourth day on the trail, he ate the last of his salt pork and the last remaining flap-jack from his tow-sack. He'd have to find food soon.

He didn't have a penny to his name, so it would do no good to stop at a store along the way, even if he found one.

He shot a rabbit the following afternoon. He cleaned and dressed it, washed it in the little stream beside his camp for the night, and skewered it over his fire. He ate the entire rabbit at one sitting.

With his hunger temporarily satisfied, he sat beside his campfire. He withdrew the hunting knife he had taken from the robber and examined it closely. It was a heavy, bone-handled knife with a blade that he guessed to be at least eight inches long. It was well-made and honed to razor-sharpness.

He rose, reversed the knife in his hand, grasped it by the blade, and flung it toward the ground. It landed, handle-first. He picked it up and tried again, this time twisting his wrist more. The sharp blade buried itself in the soft ground. Again and again he practiced until he could hit a small twig on the ground, cutting it in two. From that time forward, he spent several hours each night practicing by the light of his campfire, becoming more proficient at throwing the knife with each passing day. He learned that by throwing it from the handle, he could exert more power and throw it harder and get his throw off faster.

Late in the afternoon of the eighth day on the trail, he reined up at the edge of a small community. The sign identified it as *Mt. Pleasant.* He knew he had to have food of some kind. His stomach was cramping, he was so hungry. He hadn't eaten in three days. He heeled Ole Tom forward.

Several weathered, slat-board buildings lined the single, dusty street. A small, fresh-running stream skirted the community. He rode by a mercantile store, a saloon, a small café, and several other buildings. When he came to a livery stable, he reined up near a stooped old fellow sitting out front, whittling on a piece of wood.

"*Howdy,*" J. C. greeted.

"Good day to you, boy," the old man replied in a squeaky, high-pitched voice.

"Just passing through looking for work," J. C. said. "Know anybody that might be hiring?"

"You're a tad young to be looking for work, boy. What kind of work you looking for?"

"Anything to earn enough for a meal."

The old fellow stared intently at J. C. for a long minute, obviously taking his measure before answering.

J. C. had always been big for his age. Even at almost fourteen, he was already almost a head taller than a full-grown man. His long, cornsilk-colored hair hung to his wide shoulders. His arm muscles were hard from the farm work he had done all his life. He had friendly, sky-blue eyes.

"I got four stalls inside that need cleaning out. I'll give you fifty cents for a day's work."

"Mister, you got yourself a hand," J. C. said, quickly sliding off his mule.

"You can turn your mule in the corral. There's a pitchfork back there somewhere.

You can sleep in the hayloft tonight, if you're of a mind."

"I'm obliged. My name's J. C."

"I'm Rufus McCray. Where you hail from, boy?"

"Here and there. Like I said, just passing through."

"Uh, huh. Sorta figured as much."

J. C. leaned his rifle against the inside wall beside the door and untied his tow sacks. He turned Ole Tom into the corral, found the pitchfork, and went to work.

The stalls looked like they hadn't been cleaned in months. The manure was crusted and hard, mixed with left-over straw and tromped down by untold hooves. It was hard work prying it loose and heaping it into a big pile at the front of each stall.

Sweat soaked his ragged clothes, and the piles got higher and higher. He found a small, flat-bed wheelbarrow and hauled the piles of manure mixture out behind the livery. From time to time the liveryman walked by, paused to watch him work, and then moved on without so much as a word.

When full dark forced him to stop, he had two stalls completely finished. He went to the water trough and washed his face and hands. While he was washing, Mr. McCray walked up.

"You're a good hand, boy," the man said, handing him fifty cents. "Go on over to the café and have some supper. Tell Alice you're the one I was telling her about awhile ago."

"Thanks, Mr. McCray. I'll finish the other two stalls first thing in the morning."

"Pitch your mule some hay into the corral before you go. I expect he could use something to eat, too."

J. C. cut him a wide grin and went to do as he suggested.

Lamplight bled through the single window of the café and painted an orange square on the dusty street. J. C. opened the door and stepped inside.

There were no other customers in the small place. A heavy-set, middle age lady with an apron tied around her waist emerged from the kitchen and sized him up with a single glance.

"Bet you're the boy old Rufus was telling me about, ain't you?"

"'Spect so, ma'am."

"Have a seat somewhere. I got pot roast, stewed potatoes, cabbage, and cornbread; that suit you?"

"Sounds mighty good, ma'am," he told her, scraping out a chair and sitting down.

"Rufus says you're a good worker. I could use some help, if you're interested."

"Yes, ma'am, I shore am!"

"I need someone to clean off the tables, wash the dishes, keep the place swept and mopped; that sort of thing. It's hard work. Still interested?"

"Yes, ma'am. I surely am. Never knowed nothing 'cept hard work."

"I'll pay you fifty cents a day and all you can eat. Sound fair?"

"Ma'am, you might want to think about that. I'm a pretty big eater."

"I think we can handle that," she chuckled. "What's your name?"

"J. C. Holderfield."

"I'm Alice Bradshaw. Nice to meet you, J. C."

"It's my pleasure, Mrs. Bradshaw."

"It's *Miss* Bradshaw. I ain't married, but just call me Alice; everybody in town does. Do you drink coffee?"

"No, ma'am, just water."

"What about milk?"

"Yes, ma'am. I drink milk. We had a Jersey milk cow at home."

"Where's your parents?"

"They're both passed on."

"Oh, I'm sorry. How old are you, J. C.?"

"I'm almost fourteen, ma'am."

"You look older. You're taller than most grown men."

"Yes, ma'am, everybody says I'm big for my age."

"Let me go back and fetch your supper. It won't take but a minute."

The nice lady hurried back to the kitchen and returned shortly with a plate leaking food over the sides. She also brought a large glass of milk.

J. C. tore into the food like a half-starved wolf. The nice lady busied herself back in the kitchen until he had cleaned his plate and drank the last swallow of milk.

"There's more if you can hold it," she said, smiling.

"No, ma'am. That was plenty. It was mighty good, too; most likely the best I can ever recall."

"Think you could find room for a piece of apple pie?"

His eyes went wide, and a country smile rainbowed his mouth.

"Yes, ma'am. I 'spect I could."

She set a large slab of apple pie and another glass of milk in front of him and returned his smile.

"When you finish up over at the livery, just come on over and go to work."

"I'm shore much obliged, Miss Alice, ma'am."

Both J. C. and his mule went to bed with a full stomach that night for the first time in as long as he could remember.

The next morning, J. C. was up and working before good daylight. He finished piling the manure from the last two stalls, and then carted it outside in the wheelbarrow.

He was wheeling out the last load when Mr. McCray walked up. The liveryman inspected the stalls and nodded his head approvingly.

"You done a good job, boy. I hear you're going to work in the café."

"Yes, sir, Miss Alice gave me a job. She's shore a nice lady."

"Well, she's a mighty fine woman. She'll do right by you."

"Mr. McCray, sir, if you ever have anything else you need done, I could do it at night after I get done at the café. You wouldn't have to pay me since you're nice enough to let me sleep in the hayloft."

"You're a good worker, son. You'll go far."

J. C. thought about the liveryman's words as he washed up in the watering trough, scratched Ole Tom on the nose, and hurried off to the café.

The little café was packed when J. C. arrived. Miss Alice was running her legs off trying to cook the lunch orders, keep the coffee cups full, and carry the orders out to the hungry customers.

Without being told, J. C. grabbed the blackened coffee pot and made the rounds, refilling the customers' cups. They all smiled and nodded their thanks. Their smiles made him feel real good.

The rush lasted a couple of hours before the last customer left.

"Thanks, J. C.," Alice said. "You were a big help. Now sit down and I'll fix you some lunch."

"You don't have to do that, ma'am. I need to clear the dishes off all these tables and get busy washing them."

"There's plenty of time for that. Sit down. A growing boy like you needs three square meals a day."

Life was good.

Summer passed swiftly and the days got shorter. Winter set in with a vengeance in the Tennessee mountains.

He worked and ate at the café, slept in the hayloft of the livery, and did occasional odd jobs for Mr. McCray at night to pay for sleeping there and letting his mule board free.

Each night after he finished up at the café, he spent several hours out behind the livery, practicing with his knife. He had progressed to the point that he could now throw it from the handle with accuracy and hit a small circle scratched on the back wall of the livery.

He managed to save enough from his wages at the café to buy himself a pair of new bib overalls and a new pair of work boots from the store for his fourteenth birthday.

He had never worn anything on his feet in his whole life and felt like a real *grown-up* when he walked from the store with them on—that's when he saw him.

He was riding up the street on a grey mare. The shiny badge on his chest flashed in the setting sun—it was the lawman from Pikesville. A sudden rush of fear surged through J. C.!

What was he doing here? J. C. thought, as he ducked back inside the store. *How did he find me?*

He watched as the lawman rode on up the street. *What should I do? Do I stay and hope he don't recognize me? After all, it's been over a year. No, he wouldn't be here if he didn't already know I was here. If he catches me, he'll put me in jail for burning the house. Bad as I hate to leave, I've got no other choice.*

CHAPTER III

It was dusky-dark.

He had slipped to the back door of the café. He quickly explained to Miss Alice what had happened and why he had to leave. She begged him not to go.

"Don't go, J. C.," she pleaded. "We'll explain to him and get it worked out somehow."

"He wouldn't listen, Miss Alice," J. C. told her, with tears leaking out his eyes. "Mr. Glover's a hard man. He's the one that sent the lawman after me."

"But you've become like a son to me, J. C.," she said, with tears in her eyes.

"I'm obliged, Miss Alice, for all you've done for me."

They hugged *goodbye*. Alice pressed a double eagle gold piece into his hand.

"Take that. You'll need it wherever you go."

"You don't have to do that, Miss Alice," he protested. "You've been more'n good to me already."

Ole Tom was well-fed and ready for the trail when J. C. swung his leg across his back. He gripped his Kentucky rifle in one hand and the reins in the other as he shot a worried glance over his shoulder and heeled his mule out the back door of the livery.

He looked back just once. A huge lump lodged in his throat and a tear breeched his eye-lids as he thought about all the friends he was leaving behind.

"A man's gotta do what a man's gotta do," his pa always said.

Forcing his head around, he fixed a determined gaze on the trail ahead.

He rode all night, stopping only when he came upon a creek or stream where he paused to water his mule and scoop a drink for himself.

Daylight found him many miles away from Mount Pleasant, but still he rode on, wanting to put as many miles between him and the lawman as possible.

At noon, he paused at a small stream to water his mule. It was surrounded by a thick grove of willow trees. He decided to hide himself and his mule in the trees and take a short nap.

It was dark when he woke. He quickly shook off the momentary feeling of fright, and mounting again, he rode another night away.

His stomach was screaming out for food; he had already eaten the last of the food Miss Alice had packed for him.

Late that afternoon, he was riding along a well-travelled road through the mountains. The weather was overcast and a chilly wind out of the north whipped at him. He untied his blanket from the top of his two tow sacks and wrapped it around his shoulders.

Up ahead, he saw a log cabin that looked like a trading post or store of some kind. A long tendril of smoke trailed upward from a rock chimney.

Maybe I can buy something to eat there, he thought.

Three horses stood hip-shod at the hitching rails in front of the building. He reined his mule to a stop, tied him to one of the hitching rails alongside a black gelding with a wide-seat saddle and a set of black saddlebags tied behind it. With his rifle in one hand, J. C. walked inside. Four men were hunkered around a pot-belly stove near the back of the store. They all looked up and fixed a silent, hard look at J. C. as he walked in.

"Can I hep ye?" a big, burly, whiskered fellow asked.

"Yes, sir, I need a slab of salt pork, if you have it?"

"I got it. You got the money to pay fer it?"

"Yes, sir."

The big fellow lazily pushed upright and sauntered over to a wooden box, raised the lid, and pulled out a large slab of meat.

"How much of this you want?" he asked, picking up a long knife from the counter.

"About half of it," J. C. told him.

The man sliced the slab of meat in two pieces.

"What else you need?"

"Got any jerky?" J. C. asked.

"Got deer jerky, no beef."

"I'll take a bundle of the deer jerky."

The man reached back into the wooden box and pulled out a bundle of jerky.

"Anything else?"

"Yes, sir, I need a horn of black powder."

The man pulled a cow-horn of powder from a shelf and laid it on top of the counter.

"That'll be two dollars."

J. C. reached into his pocket, withdrew two silver dollars, and laid them on the counter. He gathered up his purchases and headed for the door. As he did, he glanced at the three men still sitting by the stove; all were eyeing him closely.

All three looked like rough mountain men. One was particularly mean-looking. He was tall and skinny with long, bushy hair that was partially covered by a coonskin cap. He wore a long, deerskin jacket with colorful beadwork and fringe along the sleeves and bottom. It reached almost to his knees. It was the fanciest jacket J. C. had ever seen.

J. C. stowed his purchases in one of his tow sacks, untied Ole Tom, and swung onto the mule's back.

The weather was getting worse. The wind was picking up and a black cloud was rolling in from the north. It was gonna be a cold, wet night.

As he rode, he searched for a place that would offer some kind of shelter. A small mountain stream with a high bank that had washed out offered the best chance for some shelter from the rain that was sure to come. He reined Ole Tom off the trail and swung down.

Using his knife, he cut several low limbs from a cedar tree and placed them on the floor of his washout under the overhang. He dragged several dead limbs over near his dugout and built a fire in the middle of the protected space. Satisfied with his home for the night, he watered his mule and unloaded his tow sacks, placing them at the very back of his washed out, shallow cave.

He sliced off two chunks of salt pork, speared them with a sharp stick, and held them over his fire until they were crispy-black.

Darkness arrived at the same time as a driving rain. A stiff wind drove the rain before it and soaked the cedar branches of his small washout. He wrapped his blanket about his shoulders and settled against the back wall to listen to the rain.

Ole Tom rumbled a low snort from deep within his belly. Something had disturbed him—he had company! He picked up his Kentucky long rifle and checked to make sure it was loaded. He listened intently for another sound.

"Hello, the camp!" a gruff voice called from the darkness.

"What you want?" J. C. asked.

"Saw your fire. We're chilled to the bone. You got coffee on?"

"No."

"Can we ride in and warm up a bit?"

"Ain't room enough for nobody 'cept me," J. C. hollered back, using one of the wet cedar limbs to douse his campfire.

For a time, the darkness was deep and silent. Then the voice called again, this time much closer.

"That ain't neighborly!" The voice was gruffer and more sinister. "'Specially on a night like this."

J. C. didn't like the sound of the man's voice. He raked back the striker on his rifle.

Even in the thick darkness, the vague, shadowy outlines of three men appeared at the edge of the trees across the small stream. Each one held a rifle in his hands.

"Don't come any closer!" J. C. warned. "I got a gun. I'll shoot!"

Without warning, one of the men's rifles exploded. The muzzle flash lit the area for a split second, revealing the three men clearly. J. C. heard the ball slap into the dirt wall only inches from his face.

Before the muzzle flash from across the stream died away, J. C. threw his rifle butt to his shoulder and fired. A high-pitched scream sounded from the darkness.

"I'm hit!" the surprised voice screamed. "That kid done shot me!"

Running footsteps sounded from the darkness, but they were running *toward* him, not *away!*

J. C. rolled to his right in the small space of the washout, just in time. Two rifles blasted from the darkness. Two rifle balls smacked into the back wall of the washout directly behind the space he had just vacated.

Both of his attackers were splashing through the shallow water of the stream directly in front of his wash out. It was too late to reload. He snatched the big hunting knife from its scabbard, grasping the handle just like he had practiced so many times.

A shadowy form in a coonskin cap appeared from the darkness only ten feet away. J. C. drew back his arm, whipped it forward with all his might, and loosed the big knife. He saw the man stagger forward another few steps before pitching facedown onto the ground.

The third man seemed to pause a moment, looking down at his companion, and let out a blood-curdling scream that sent shivers down J. C.'s spine. The man charged the remaining few feet that separated them.

J. C. reversed his rifle, butt forward, and swung it with all his might as the man came within range. The shock of the impact radiated up J. C.'s arms. He heard the sharp crack of bone as the heavy wood of the rifle butt struck the man directly in the face. In the faint light, he saw blood and bone splay into the air. The man toppled over backwards and didn't move.

For a long moment, J. C. sat motionless, breathing heavily. It was his first fight! He had just killed three men! His stomach rebelled—and emptied his supper.

He sat beside the small campfire the remainder of the night—reliving the events he had just experienced.
I had no choice, he reasoned. *There's no doubt they meant to kill me. It was me or them. But then why am I feeling guilty for killing three men?*

Sometime during the long night, the rain stopped. Dawn finally arrived. J. C. crawled from his small dugout and looked around. He pulled the heavy blade from the lifeless body of the man in the coonskin cap and fringed coat. It made a sickly, sucking sound as it came out. He gathered up the three rifles and looked them over carefully. They were good ones; it would be a shame to just throw them away. He decided to keep them, but how could he carry three additional rifles?

After he had disposed of the bodies and was packing to leave, an idea struck him. He cut two short sections from one of the robbers' lariats and tied one to the front of his saddle and the other to the back.

He lifted his right stirrup and fender and placed one of the robbers' rifles against the ropes and looped the rope around it, securing it with a slip knot. He placed the second one about six inches below the first, and again looped the ropes around it and tied it in place. He did the same with the third rifle, as well as his own.

When he finished, he lowered the stirrup and fender and looked at his handiwork and was pleased. If needed quickly, he would be able to get to all four rifles, giving him four times the firepower he had before.

The best part of a week later, J. C. rode into the outskirts of Memphis, Tennessee. He was atop a solid black, high-stepping gelding. Ole Tom, his Missouri mule, and two extra saddle horses followed on lead lines.

J. C. wore the fancy, deerskin coat and coonskin cap, once owned by the late *would-be* highwayman who was now buried along with his two companions under the caved-in washout, several days on his back trail.

Memphis was without a doubt the largest town he had ever seen. Riding through the busy streets, he felt small and insignificant. He paused to ask a fellow driving a big freight wagon where he could find the nearest livery.

"Just keep riding, sonny," the man said, without slowing down. "You'll run right into it."

Sure enough, another quarter-hour later, he saw a large livery and blacksmith business up ahead. A giant of a man in a leather apron was shoeing a grey plow horse when J. C. reined up.

"Afternoon," J. C. greeted.

The big hostler glanced up from his job, with half-a-dozen horseshoe nails between his bearded lips. The man nodded a greeting while eyeing the four rifles secured along his mount's right side. J. C. sat his saddle and waited until the man finished shoeing the hoof.

"How can I help you?" the hostler asked, studying J. C.'s frame from head to toe.

"Know where I could sell two horses?"

The man glanced briefly at the horses.

"Maybe so. Where'd you get 'em?"

"My folks passed on and I'm traveling."

"What you want for them?"

"What you offering?"

The hostler stepped over and looked the horses over with a long look. He checked both of their mouths, ran his hand along their sides, and raised their hooves.

"Not much market for horses these days. I'd give you thirty apiece for them—no more. Give you forty for the mule."

"Give me forty apiece for the horses and we've got a deal," J. C. told him. "The mule ain't for sale."

"Can't do it, son. I'd be losing money."

J. C. nodded and reined his gelding around as if to ride away. He got only a few steps.

"Alright, alright! Forty apiece, but you got to throw in the saddles and bridles," the hostler said. "You drive a hard bargain."

The man dug into his work pants and withdrew four double eagle gold pieces. J. C. put the money into his pocket.

"You got a cheap packsaddle for sale?"

"Yep. Just happened to have."

The man stepped inside a tack room and emerged with a canvas packsaddle.

"How much?"

"Oh, five dollars ought to cover it."

"I'll take it."

"Shore toting an awful lot of firepower there," the liveryman said.

"Lots of bad people hereabouts," J. C. said, as he girded the packsaddle in place on his mule and tied the three extra rifles to it. "I saw a big river over yonder a ways."

"Yep. That's the mighty Mississippi. That's Arkansas on the other side."

"How would a fellow get across it?"

"Two streets down, turn right and keep going. You'll come to a ferry boat that will take you across."

"Much obliged, Mister."

He came across a mercantile store in the next block and decided he ought to restock his trail supplies. He reined up, climbed down, and wrapped the reins around the hitching rail out front.

"Good afternoon," the store owner greeted.

"*Howdy,*" J. C. said, sweeping a look around the store.

He spotted a long-tailed, canvas duster and lifted it from the rack.

"Is it alright if I try it on?"

"Why shore, help yourself."

J. C. sleeved into the garment over the top of his deerskin jacket. It fit him perfectly. It buttoned up the front and was split to his waist in both the front and back for riding. He figured it would be good to keep both rain and dust off.

"How much?" he asked.

"Four dollars."

"I'll take it," he told the man. "I need a slab of salt pork, a tin of coffee, one of them Indian blankets, and a ground sheet. Oh, yeah, I need a small skillet and coffee pot, too."

The storekeeper gathered the supplies and laid them on the counter.

"That'll make it nine dollars," the man said.

J. C. dug the money out of his pocket and handed it to the store-keeper.

"Where you headed, young fellow?"

"Anywhere I can find work."

"Fellow was in here a couple of days ago headed for Texas. He said there was lots of jobs to be had in Texas."

"Might give it some thought," J. C. said.

J. C. gathered his purchases and left the store. He stuffed his supplies into his packsaddle. He rolled his two blankets and the ground sheet and tied the roll behind his saddle. Last, he tied his new duster over the top of his bedroll, gathered the lead line to his mule, and stepped into the saddle of his gelding.

The sun was setting when J. C. reined up near the loading ramp of the ferry boat. The large, flat-bottom barge was on a return trip from the far bank and was near the middle of the wide, swift-running river.

He stepped to the ground and watched. A long rope was stretched from one bank to the other and secured to a large tree on both sides. The rope was threaded through an iron eye anchored to the barge. Two giant, bare-chested black men pulled the barge along with the rope. A third man, who J. C. took to be the owner, stood on the boat nearby, overseeing the progress.

The big barge slowly pulled into the bank. The black men lowered a gangplank and the owner stepped ashore.

"You going to the other side, young fellow?"

"Yes, sir."

"It's my last trip for the day. For you and your animals, the fee is one dollar."

J. C. pulled the money from his pocket and handed it to the man. He led his gelding and pack mule up the gang plank.

"You peddling rifles?" the man asked.

"No, sir, them ain't for sale."

"Where you headed?"

"Texas."

"Long ways to Texas. You're heading into dangerous country the minute you step off my barge. There's more outlaws and Indians in the country you're heading into

than fleas on a yard dog. Apt-as-not, you'll be needing
them rifles where you're heading."

"I'm much obliged."

The heavily-muscled black men strained at the thick
rope, slowly moving the big barge through the water. As
he watched the water rush past the heavy barge,
contrasting emotions surged through him.

Youthful excitement of new adventures was
dampened by uneasiness about the future. He had already
experienced how dangerous the world could be for a
young boy traveling alone.

Living a sheltered life on a farm in the mountains of
Tennessee, he had grown up trusting everyone. Now, he
was learning that not everyone was trustworthy. He
determined then and there that from now on, he wouldn't
trust anybody until they earned his trust.

J. C. rocked forward when the big barge jarred into
the bank on the far side of the Mississippi River. The
wooden gangplank was lowered and he led his horse and
mule from the barge.

The ferry boat owner lifted a hand and waved as J. C.
took his Kentucky long rifle in hand, toed a stirrup, and
swung a leg over his saddle. He returned the man's wave
and did a half-hitch of Ole Tom's lead line around his
saddle horn. He gathered the reins and heeled the black
gelding forward.

"Got no idea what your name is," he said out loud to
his mount. "Reckon I'll call you *Blackie*. Yeah, that fits
you. Okay, *Blackie,* let's me and you see where this here
road takes us."

The road was well-traveled and wallowed out from
untold heavy wagons that had passed this way. Both sides
of the road were choked with heavy growths of willow

trees. The land was flatter than the flapjacks Miss Alice served back in Mt. Pleasant.

The thought of Mt. Pleasant and the friends he had left behind brought a lump into his throat. He would have been happy to settle down there—but his past caught up with him—he had to move on.

He settled easily into the gentle rhythm of his new horse's gait and the miles passed quickly beneath his high-stepping hooves. Now and then he met a wagon heading toward Memphis. On those occasions, he lifted a hand in greeting and the occupants returned it, friendly-like. He rode steady for three days.

CHAPTER IV

The country through which he was riding was vastly different from any he had ever known. Gone were the high mountain ranges and thick forests. The country he rode through was mostly flat, with occasional rolling hills. The tall pine and cedar were replaced by scrawny blackjack, willow, sycamore, and oak trees.

At mid-afternoon of the fifth day since crossing the river, he came across a slat-board farm house that sat in a stand of tall oak trees back off the road a piece. It reminded him of the one he had grown up in.

A dug well with a pulley suspended over it caught his attention and reminded him that his canteen was dry. He reined into the yard of the small, box-like house and called out.

"Hello, the house!"

A young girl appeared in the open doorway. She had long, stringy, blondish hair and wore a drab, flour-sack dress that hung loosely on her frail-looking frame.

She'd be right pretty if she was cleaned up a bit, he thought.

"Wondering if you'd mind if I draw up a bucket of water from your well?" he asked loudly.

"Help yourself," she hollered back, staring uneasily at him.

He reined up beside the well and stepped to the ground. The girl still stood, leaning against the side of the open door. She appeared to be young, probably not much older than he was.

He took hold of the well rope and lowered the bucket into the well. He twisted his wrist to allow water to fill the bucket and then drew it from the well. A gourd dipper hung on the frame. He dipped it into the bucket and drank deeply. The water was fresh and cool. He drank three dippers full before filling his canteen.

"You can water your animals, if you're of a mind," the girl offered.

"Much obliged, ma'am. That's mighty nice of you." He drew several more buckets and filled the nearby wooden water trough. He allowed his horse and mule to slake their thirst. While his animals drank, he glanced around.

The house was in disrepair. The front door hung catawampus on one hinge. Where a window should be was nothing but a gaping hole. The door of the small barn nearby was completely off and lying on the ground. The roof had a large hole in it where several shingles were missing. A broken-down farm wagon sat in the runway of the barn. A wheel lay on the ground nearby.

Several poles were down from the split rail corral that held a gaunt-looking milk cow. Several red laying hens scratched in the yard for their meal. The small garden spot needed working and where there was once a woodpile, only a few small scraps remained. All these signs of neglect told him there wasn't a man around or, if there was, he wasn't much of one. All these things he observed in a single, sweeping glance.

"Who lives here besides you?" he asked.

"Nobody but me and my pa, but he's laid up in bed," she told him. "My ma died two years ago, now Pa's all crippled up and can't get out of bed."

"I'm real sorry, ma'am."

"Where you be headed?" she asked, venturing from the doorway and sitting down on the wooden steps.

"Don't rightly know, ma'am. Texas I reckon."

"Never been to Texas," she said. "They say it's a long way off."

"I reckon so," he said.

"Never been much of anywhere," she said, sadness evident in her voice. "We went to Memphis once, but that was a long time ago when I was real little."

"None of my business, ma'am, but with your pa laid up, how do you get by?"

"I make do."

"I got some time," he said. "If your pa has no objections, I could drag up some logs and chop you some firewood, if you like?"

"We got no money to pay you."

"Don't expect no pay."

"That would be mighty nice of you, mister. What's your name?"

"J. C."

"My name's Opal Sullivan. My ma said she named me after a precious stone she read about that rich folks wear. She always called me *Precious*, like the opal."

"Pretty name," he said. "Mind me asking how old you are?"

"I'm fifteen."

"You're older than me. I ain't but fourteen."

"Really? You look a lot older than that. You look plumb growed up."

"Why don't you go ask your pa if it's okay if I drag up a few logs?"

"Ain't no need asking him. Besides, he's more'n likely asleep."

"If you're sure it'll be okay, I'll turn my horse into the corral while I use my mule to drag up some logs."

"You need some help?"

"No, ma'am, but thanks for offering."

The girl watched him while he led his horse and mule into the corral. He unsaddled his horse and removed the packsaddle from Ole Tom. He saw a set of harness and log chains hanging on the wall inside the barn and rigged it up on his mule.

Shouldering the ax and walking behind the big Missouri mule, he headed for a nearby line of woods. He located a long, weathered log, lopped off a few stubby limbs, and secured the log chain to it. He dragged it back to the house and returned to the woods for another. By late afternoon, he had a large collection of logs piled beside the house.

It was a warm afternoon. The sun was kissing the western horizon—too late to start chopping firewood—he'd ask about sleeping in the barn tonight and do the chopping tomorrow.

He was sweaty and dirty by the time he unharnessed Ole Tom and hobbled both his mule and horse on a patch of green grass near the barn. He drew some water, filled the water trough, and shrugged from his sweaty shirt to wash himself.

A long, thin tendril of smoke trailed upward toward a darkening sky. A sweet-smelling aroma wafted across a soft evening breeze from the house.

The girl emerged as he was sleeving into his shirt. She was carrying a milk bucket and heading toward the corral where the milk cow waited. She paused a short distance away. He saw her glance at his uncovered chest and then blush and look quickly away, seemingly embarrassed.

"Supper's almost ready," she told him.

"Weren't no need to do that for my sake," J. C. said.

"I wanted to. Soon as I milk the cow, I'll be putting it on the table."

"I'll milk the cow for you," he volunteered. "I always did the milking at home."

"Why'd you leave home?"

"My folks are both passed on. No reason to stay."

"I got a older brother somewheres, but don't know where he's at. Haven't heard from him since I was little."

"I see," J. C. said, but didn't.

He reached out for the milk bucket. The girl handed it to him and turned back toward the house.

"Come on up to the house when you're done," she said over a shoulder. "Supper'll be ready."

He finished milking the cow and took time to hobble her on the grass close to his horse before heading for the house. The closer he got, the better the food smelled. He climbed the steps and stepped inside.

Opal was setting the last bowl of food on a slat-board table. A wooden bench sat on either side of the table. J. C.'s gaze migrated to a large bowl of crispy-looking fried chicken. Another was full of biscuits, and yet another contained flour gravy.

"That shore looks fittin'," he said, handing her the bucket of milk.

She took it and offered a pretty smile in return.

"Much obliged for doin' the milking. You want some milk with supper?"

"That'd be good," he said.

"Set up to the table, then, and I'll fetch you a glass."

He stepped over the bench and sat down. A shiny knife and fork lay beside a pretty plate that had flowers on it.

"Mighty nice of you to do all this," he told her.

"Weren't nothin'."

"It is to me. I ain't used to something this nice. I usually eat my own cooking right outta the frying pan."

The girl brought a large glass of milk and set it beside his plate before sitting down on the bench across the table from him.

"Help yourself," she told him, staring intently at him.

"These shore are pretty plates and stuff," he told her, embarrassed by her stare.

"They were my ma's. She brought them all the way from Alabama when her and Pa moved here."

J. C. broke open two biscuits and covered them with a large helping of gravy. He selected a chicken leg from the platter and took a big bite.

"Umm, this shore is good!" he said around a mouthful of chicken. "Best I ever ate!"

Opal smiled appreciatively, but didn't offer to fill her plate. She just sat watching him eat. Glancing up, he saw her staring at him with an unwavering look.

"Ain't you gonna eat?" he asked.

"I will later. I like watching you eat. It makes me feel good."

He felt himself blush and ducked his head to hide his embarrassment.

"When—when does your pa eat?"

"I'll take him something after we're done. He wants to meet you."

"Reckon he'd care if I sleep in the barn tonight?"

"Why would he care?"

"Don't know, but I'll ask him just to make shore. Where do you folks buy your supplies?"

"We don't have no money to buy nothin'. We make do. Fort Gibson is a half-day's ride northwest, the other side of the Brushy Mountains, but that's too far for me to walk. Besides, I can't leave Pa long enough to make a trip like that. The Jameses live up the road a piece. They're nice folks, but they ain't much better off then we are. They let me breed our cow to their bull every year."

"I'll chop you up some firewood tomorrow," he told her, glancing up from his supper.

"Why you want to go to Texas?" she asked.

J. C. shrugged his shoulders without looking up from his supper.

"I don't know. Everybody's gotta be somewhere, I reckon. They say there's lots of jobs in Texas."

"You could stay here with us."

He wrinkled his forehead and glanced up at her with a questioning look.

"Why'd I want to do that?"

"I don't know. You said everybody's gotta be someplace. Might as well be here as anywhere."

He shook his head and took a long swallow of milk.

"I might stay a few days just to help out around the place if it's alright with your pa."

That brought a wide smile to Opal's face and a vigorous nod of her head. She broke open a biscuit and spooned a helping of gravy over it. J. C. reached for another piece of chicken.

After another plateful of biscuits and gravy, he drained the last of his milk from the glass and swiped his mouth with his shirt sleeve. Opal filled a clean plate with food and pushed up from the table.

"I'm gonna take Pa some supper."

"I'll come with you," he said, rising to his feet.

The small, lean-to bedroom was barely big enough to contain the bed in which Mr. Sullivan lay, but it was clean and smelled fresh. The bearded man had his eyes closed when they stepped into the room. J. C. judged the man to be straddling forty, give or take. He was covered to his chest with a blanket. The top of his clean-looking, red long-johns showed above the blanket.

"Brought you some supper, Pa."

The man opened his eyes and glanced, first at his daughter, and then settled a searching gaze upon J. C.

"Opal told me you drug up some timber for firewood," he said. "I'm beholden to you."

"Weren't nothing. I'll set in chopping it up come morning. Is it okay for me to bed down in your barn?"

"Don't know any reason why not."

Opal spread a dishtowel across her pa's chest and placed the plate of food on it.

"She told me your name, but I forgot," the man said, picking up the fork and filling his mouth.

"Name's J. C Holderfield."

The man nodded, glancing again at J. C.

"Mighty decent of you to do for us when we can't pay you."

"That supper was pay enough."

"How old are you, boy?"

"I'm fourteen, sir."

"Don't *sir* me. Name's *Lester.* I'd be obliged if you'd call me Lester."

J. C. nodded.

"I'll be goin' and let you eat your supper," J. C. said, turning and leaving the room. He left the house and headed toward the barn.

It was a clear night—clear and chilly. A full moon lit the night almost as bright as day. He entered the barn and untied his bedroll from the back of his saddle. There was a ladder that led up to a small hayloft. He climbed it and spread his bedroll on the small bit of hay that remained. Soft footsteps down below caught his attention. A head appeared over the top of the ladder—it was Opal.

"Brought you a quilt," she said. "It gets kinda cold this time of year."

"I've got my blankets," he told her, "but I'm obliged."

She carefully placed the folded quilt beside his bedroll and continued to stand on the ladder.

"Pa likes you."

"How you know that?" he asked.

"Cause he said so. Tell me 'bout Texas and what you're gonna do when you get there?"

"Don't know nothing 'bout Texas. Never been there. Never been much of anywhere 'cept Pikesville, Tennessee."

"You got a girl back in Pikesville, Tennessee?"

"Well, no, not really. There was this one girl I liked, but her pa didn't like me much. Only time I ever seen her was in school and church on Sundays."

"Was she pretty?"

He pursed his lips and shrugged.

"I reckon."

"Wish I was pretty," she said sadly.

He swallowed, and then swallowed again, not knowing what to say.

"I better be goin,' I reckon," she said, scrambling down the ladder.

For a long time he lay there on his blanket, staring up through the dim darkness at the roof of the barn. Night sounds filled the surrounding silence. Confused thoughts filled his mind until sleep carried him away into a strange world of dreams.

A rooster crowing jerked him awake. He sat upright, for a moment confused at his surroundings. He combed his fingers through his long hair and set his coonskin cap in place. He climbed down the ladder and walked to the water trough. He sloshed water on his face and scrubbed it dry with his hands while looking around.

Smoke billowed from the rock chimney. That meant Opal was already awake. The thought of her brought back memories of the night before.

She is pretty, he told himself. For a long moment, he stood, remembering the innocent blush of her face, the pretty little smile, and her jade colored eyes that somehow looked sad most of the time.

The faint smell of frying salt pork reached him. He glanced toward where he had hobbled his horse, mule, and the cow. They were munching peacefully on shocks of green grass. The cow raised her head long enough to let out a long bawl, announcing it was time to milk her.

He headed for the house to get the milk bucket. He paused at the front door and knocked softly.

"Come in," Opal's soft voice called from inside.

He opened the door and stepped inside.

She stood in front of the stove in a white housecoat that fell to her ankles, and covering a white nightgown. Her face looked rosy from scrubbing.

"Mornin'," she said cheerfully.

"Mornin'," he replied. "I come to get the milk bucket."

"It's right over there," she told him, pointing with a nod of her head. "Breakfast will be ready by the time you finish milking."

He picked up the bucket and nodded before stepping hurriedly from the room. All the time he was milking, his mind was on the picture of her standing there, all fresh-scrubbed and morning fresh.

He finished milking, returned the cow to the little patch of grass, washed his hands and face in the watering trough, and headed for the smell of breakfast from the house.

Opal had changed clothes and had on a pretty, colorful, flour-sack dress that had yellow flowers on it. Her blonde hair was pulled back and tied with a long, shiny, yellow ribbon. Her jade-green eyes sparkled as he stared at her for a long moment.

Breakfast was on the table. He set the bucket of milk on a small work table against the wall.

He slanted another glance at her as he took his place at the table. She had a fixed look at him with a wide smile on her face.

"What?" he asked, with a questioning look.

"Nothing, I was just looking at you," she replied, blushing at getting caught staring at him.

He shrugged and scooped three eggs from the platter onto his plate. She scooted a large plate of biscuits closer to him.

"There's still some sorghum molasses left if you like it on your biscuits," she suggested. "Pa likes it on his."

"I do, too," he said, pouring half of the remaining molasses onto his plate, careful to save the rest for her pa. "Been thinking. After I get some wood chopped, I'm gonna ride over to that town you told me about and pick up a few things."

"Really? What sort of *things*? You mean things for your trip to Texas?"

"Well, yeah, but some supplies for you and your pa, too."

"That would be mighty nice of you, but you don't have to do that. We don't have money for supplies."

"I know, but I want to."

"How long will you be gone?" she asked.

"You said it was about a half-day's ride, didn't you? I could leave first thing in the morning and be back by dark."

"Can I go with you?" she asked with her eyes, as well as her words.

He thought about it and decided she deserved to get away from taking care of her pa all the time.

"Would your pa be alright with you being gone that long?"

"I'll ask him, but don't see why not; he sleeps most of the time anyway."

"Well, if he says it's alright with him, it's alright with me."

A smile broke across her face that stretched nearly from ear to ear. She leaped up from her bench, rushed around the table, and planted a quick kiss on his cheek just as he forked a mouthful of eggs into his mouth.

He was so shocked by her actions, he nearly spewed the eggs from his mouth.

"Oh, thank you, J. C.!" she shouted. "I can't wait until tomorrow! What am I gonna wear?" she asked herself out loud.

"Wear what you got on," he said, after he had time to swallow his eggs. "You look mighty pretty in that."

A crimson blush flushed across her face. She looked quickly at the floor and turned her back to him, but the smile on her face belied her embarrassment.

"Guess it'll have to be, this is the only dress I got that ain't a work dress."

After breakfast, J. C. decided to walk over into the nearby woods and see if he could kill a squirrel or something for supper.

He loaded his Kentucky long rifle and set out. He found a likely place beside a small stream and sat down with his back against a large oak tree.

The early morning sun was up and warming things. His eyes got heavy and he actually dozed off a time or two. Something jerked him awake. A big buck deer stood beside the small stream no more than thirty yards away.

J. C. slowly eased his rifle to his shoulder. He carefully raked back the striker and laid his sight just behind the animal's right shoulder, took a deep breath, let it out, and squeezed the trigger.

When the lead slug struck, the large buck leaped straight up into the air and hit the ground running. It cleared the stream with a single bound and disappeared into the heavy brush across the stream.

J. C. leaped up and set out after him. He found large blood spots every few feet and followed them for several hundred yards before he found the deer. It was lying in a thicket of scrub cedar bushes.

He used his hunting knife to field dress the animal and hoisted it onto his shoulders with the feet on either side of his neck. It was a long walk back to the house. Opal was excited to see what he had killed. J. C. cut up the deer and Opal washed it beside the well.

"We'll have to cure out the meat or it will ruin," he told her. "I seen a small smokehouse behind the barn."

"Yeah, Pa used to smoke hogs in it before he got down sick, but it hasn't been used in a long time."

"I'll check it out; meantime, we'll salt it down good and bury it until we get back from Fort Gibson."

"Bury it?" she questioned.

"Yeah, I'll dig a hole and wrap the meat in a quilt or something. The cool temperature of the ground will start the curing process and keep it from spoiling until we get back."

"You're so smart," she said proudly.

Her words made him feel good.

He found a shovel and dug a large, deep hole at least six feet in the ground. They salted the meat heavily and wrapped it in a clean quilt and tied it tight with a rope. They placed it in the hole and covered it to ground level.

"That should do it," he told her, propping the shovel against the side of the house. "Now I've got wood to cut." He set in sawing the tree trunks into smaller lengths with an old saw he found in the barn. After he had a pile cut, he began splitting it into firewood. By the time the sun was touching the western horizon, he had one rick split and stacked against the side of the house.

For supper they all enjoyed large deer steaks with a big bowl of flour gravy and a pan of hot biscuits. They ate hungrily. While they ate, Opal talked excitedly about their trip to Fort Gibson.

"Pa said he guessed it'd be alright for me to go with you tomorrow."

"Good. We'll get an early start and ought to be back before dark. You can ride my horse and I'll ride Ole Tom."

"I can ride the mule," she protested. "Bet I can ride bareback as good as you can."

"Maybe," he conceded.

"You got enough money to buy supplies? We sure ain't got none."

"I got enough."

CHAPTER V

After telling her pa *goodbye* and assuring him they would be back by dark, they mounted and headed northwest. He convinced her to ride his horse while he rode Ole Tom. It was uncomfortable riding bareback with their empty packsaddle behind him.

The country was completely different from what he had traveled through since leaving Tennessee. Heavily wooded, rolling hills crowded the narrow, rutted road. Large oak and sycamore trees, thickets of scrub blackjack and cedar, and thick underbrush offered cover for all kinds of wildlife. Deer, rabbits, and squirrels scampered across the road in front of them.

Opal seemed excited about the trip. She kept up a steady stream of one-sided conversation as they rode side by side.

They reached Fort Gibson at mid-morning. It sat on the bank of a large river near the junction of another river.

The fort was a series of square block buildings made from heavy logs, connected by a walled stockade. Two, two-story gun towers stood in opposite corners. Soldiers, civilians, and Indians passed through a high gate made from heavy logs.

A cluster of twenty or so Indian lodges stood on the opposite bank of one of the rivers. Several Indian men sat around a fire smoking long pipes and they turned to stare as J. C. and Opal rode past.

They rode through the wide gate and reined up in front of the post commissary. The wide, covered porch that fronted the store had a line of wooden barrels containing all sorts of ax handles, shovels, and various tools.

Several soldiers lounged against the front of the store, passing a bottle between them and eyeing Opal with leering gazes.

J. C. slid off his mule and tied the reins to the hitching rail. He helped Opal to the ground and tied his horse beside the mule. He took Opal's arm and walked past the soldiers toward the front door of the store. One of the young soldiers mumbled a comment to the others that J. C. couldn't hear. His companions all laughed.

Half-a-dozen shoppers were rummaging through the piles of blankets, clothes, and boots piled high on long tables. Shelves from floor to ceiling were stocked with all sorts of food-stuff. Racks full of rifles stood against one wall.

A bald headed man with a full, white beard and a dirty apron tied around his waist approached them.

"Can I hep you young folks?"

"Yes, sir," J. C. replied. "We need a sack of salt, a sack of flour, cornmeal, and sugar. Give us a bag of green.

coffee beans and a twenty pound sack of dried beans and a sack of dried corn. We need three slabs of salt pork, too." He added several more items, including several tins of fresh-canned peaches. The storekeeper nodded and hurried away to gather their order while Opal looked around. J. C. saw her stop in front of a rack of ladies dresses. She stared longingly at them. He watched as she selected a pretty blue one with white lace trim around the neck and sleeves. She held it up against herself and smiled. J. C. walked over to her.

"That's right pretty," he said. "You like it?"

She nodded and returned the dress to the rack with a sad look on her face. J. C. reached a hand and retrieved the dress, handing it back to her.

"It's yours," he said.

A shocked expression covered her face. She shook her head emphatically.

"No!" she said. "I couldn't!"

"Of course you can. I want to buy it for you."

She hesitated for only a moment before pressing the dress against her body and twirling in a happy circle. The beautiful smile on her face alone was worth whatever the dress would cost, he figured.

While the storekeeper was gathering their purchases, J. C. spotted a glass-covered case containing pipes. He pointed to one and told the store man he wanted it.

"I'll need two pouches of tobacco, too."

"You smoke a pipe?" Opal asked him, with a skeptical look.

"No, but I figured your pa might like it."

He paid for their purchases, carried them outside and loaded them onto the packsaddle and tying, them securely. He couldn't help noticing the soldiers still staring at Opal.

"Hey, sonny, is she your sister?" one of the soldiers asked, stepping forward.

J. C. twisted a hard look at the man. He judged the soldier to be in his early to mid-twenties. His wide shoulders and arm muscles stretched the sleeves of his blue military shirt. He looked like the typical bully.

He decided the best thing to do was try to ignore the man. He turned back to packing his supplies.

"Hey! Don't turn your back on me! I asked you a question!"

A hot flush reddened J. C.'s throat. He slowly turned his head to focus his look at the soldier. Two others stepped closer to their companion.

"No, she ain't my sister, but I work for her pa."

The soldier pushed the bottle of whiskey toward Opal.

"Well, then, how about me and you having a little drink, pretty girl?" he asked.

Opal shook her head and backed away a few steps. The other soldiers laughed at their companion being rejected. Anger colored his face a crimson red. He lunged forward and wrapped an arm around Opal's waist and pulled her against him.

J. C. quickly stepped forward, clamped a strong hand on the soldier's arm and jerked it roughly from Opal's waist. The force of J. C.'s action spun the soldier around.

J. C. flicked a quick look at Opal to make sure she was alright. When he glanced back, he saw a big fist coming at him from the corner of his eye. It was a wide-arching haymaker that would have torn his head from his shoulders if it had landed.

He easily ducked under the blow by bending swiftly at the waist. When he straightened up, his own work-hardened fist came with him. It started just below knee level and buried wrist-deep in the soldier's stomach just below his belt buckle.

A gush of air expelled from the soldier's stomach and burst from his open mouth. The force of J. C.'s blow doubled the man forward. Using both hands, he grabbed the soldier behind the head and held it tightly as his knee shot upward with all the force he could muster.

The sickly sound of breaking bone could be heard clearly by the gathering crowd. The soldier slammed upward, his feet leaving the ground before collapsing in an unconscious and bloody heap in the dusty street.

He didn't move—but his two companions did. They rushed forward, grabbing at J. C. He dodged from their grasp. His eyes spotted a wooden barrel full of ax handles. He grabbed one and swung around to face his two attackers.

"That's enough!" a firm voice shouted.

An army officer with gold bars on his shoulders stood nearby with his hands on his hips. He was glaring at the fallen soldier's two companions.

"It was a fair fight. The corporal lost. Pick him up and get him over to the infirmary!"

The two soldiers picked up their unconscious comrade and hurried him away. The officer stepped over near J. C.

"I apologize for my man's behavior. From the sound of it, it'll be awhile before he'll be able to enjoy a meal with that broken jaw. What's your name, son?"

"J. C. Holderfield, sir."

"How old are you?"

"I'm fourteen, sir."

The officer pursed his lips and nodded his head.

"You look older. You're pretty good with your fists for fourteen. What's your friend's name?"

"Her name's Opal Sullivan, sir. She lives about a half-day's ride south of here. I work for her pa. We came to get some supplies."

"I see."

"Are we free to go, sir?"

"Don't see why not. The way I saw it, you were just defending the girl."

"Much obliged," J. C. said, reaching a hand. The officer took it and they shook hands warmly.

"Somehow, I got a feeling we'll meet again sometime," the officer said.

"Maybe so," J. C. said, nodding his head.

The sun buried itself behind the western horizon and the evening shadows invaded the land as J. C. and Opal arrived home and reined up near the barn.

"Go ahead and check on your pa," he suggested. "I'll unload our supplies and see to the stock."

Opal nodded agreement as J. C. helped her from the saddle.

"I'll just check on Pa and be right back to help with the chores."

She hurried into the house as he led their mounts into the barn to unsaddle them. He was just finishing when Opal returned, carrying the milk bucket.

He took it from her and tied the milk cow to a stall. He sat down on the small stool and began milking. Opal stood nearby watching.

"Thank you for my dress," she said.

"You're welcome. I enjoyed our trip."

"Me, too. I'm sorry about the fight."

"It wasn't your fault. You didn't do nothing."

"Where'd you learn to fight like that?"

"I don't know. I just done what needed to be done, I reckon."

"Well, you sure whipped him good. I was so proud of you."

He felt the warmth of a blush flash across his face and changed the subject.

"How was your pa?"

"He's okay. I need to go fix us all some supper. Come on up to the house when you get done."

She gathered an armload of the supplies and headed for the house. Within short minutes, smoke billowed from the rock chimney. He finished milking and hobbled the milk cow on a patch of green grass nearby.

He took time to brush down both his horse and Ole Tom before hefting the sacks of salt and flour onto his shoulders and heading for the house.

Opal was busy starting supper when he walked in. He laid the sacks of flour and salt on the kitchen work table and sat down on a bench at the table.

"Did you give your pa his pipe and tobacco?" he asked.

Opal twisted a look over her shoulder and shook her head.

"I thought you'd want to do that."

He picked up the pipe and the tobacco and went to Mr. Sullivan's bedroom. He lay there in bed with his eyes closed. J. C. stared at him for a long minute. Concern swept over him. The man had the same pale, sickly look he remembered his mother having just before she passed away. J. C. decided to give him the pipe later and had turned to go when the man suddenly opened his eyes. His voice sounded weak.

"Opal tells me you had a good trip," the man said.

"Yes, sir, we did," he said, handing the pipe and tobacco to Mr. Sullivan. "Thought you might enjoy a smoke now and again."

He glanced first at the pipe, and then up at J. C. before fixing a long look at the pipe. He caressed it with a frail hand as one would a newborn baby. A tear escaped his eyes and trailed across his cheek.

"Always wanted a pipe, but just never seemed to have the extra money. I'm much obliged, son."

"I appreciate getting to stay here awhile, Mr. Sullivan."

"You've been a big help to my daughter. She works hard to take care of me and keep things going, but it's been awfully hard on her."

"She's a fine lady."

"Opal said you're headed for Texas?"

"That's what I got in mind, yes, sir."

"You'd be welcome to stay here with us."

"That's mighty nice of you, sir, but the way I see it, that wouldn't be right. I'll stay until I get done what needs done, if that's alright with you."

"Can I ask a favor?" Mr. Sullivan asked.

"Of course."

"Don't know how much longer I got. I just worry about what will happen to my daughter after I'm gone. I know it's a lot to ask, but you're the only hope I got. Would you see she's not left here alone after my time is up?"

The question rocked J. C. right down to his bones. *How can I take responsibility for Opal? What would I do with her? Where could I leave her that she would be safe? But how can I refuse the man's dying request? What else can I do?*

"I'll see she's taken care of," he promised.

Mr. Sullivan reached a weak hand. J. C. took it and with the handshake, made a promise.

"Supper's ready!" Opal called from the other room.

"What were you and pa talking about?" Opal asked, as J. C. took his seat at the table.

"He asked me to stay here with you folks awhile."

She raised a look at him and held it as she asked, "What'd you say?"

"I told him I'd stay until I got some things done that needed doing."

"And then?"

"Then I reckon I'll go on to Texas."

Opal dropped her head and rose quickly from the bench. She rushed outside without saying a word.

J. C. sat for a long moment, staring after her, wondering what he said that upset her like that. He finally rose and went after her.

He found her standing on the porch. She was crying.

"What's wrong, Opal? What'd I say?"

She just shook her head without replying. He took her by the shoulders and gently turned her around to face him. Her tear-wet eyes refused to look at him. She stared at the floor.

Slowly, gently, he reached a curled finger to lift her chin.

"Look at me. What's wrong?"

For a long moment, he thought she wasn't going to answer. Their gazes held one another.

"I—I was just hoping—never mind," she said with a shaky voice, pulling free and rushing back into the house to her small bedroom and closing the door.

J. C. sat back down at the table. He stared at his plate, confused by Opal's sudden, tearful display of emotion.

He suddenly realized he had lost his appetite. He
rose, left the cabin, and walked slowly toward the barn.
His black gelding lifted his head from grazing and walked
to meet J. C.

He patted Blackie's neck and rubbed his nose.

The night was chilly. A cold wind was blowing from
the north and carried the smell of rain.

Looks like it's gonna be a cold, wet night, he thought.
Gathering a handful of his horse's mane, he led the
gelding into the barn and put him in a stall. He returned
with a rope and also led Ole Tom and the milk cow into
the barn.

Satisfied, he climbed the ladder to his bedroll, pried
off his boots, and lay down. For a long time he lay in the
dark, thinking.

It worried him that Opal had got upset like that, but
what worried him more was the promise he had made to
Mr. Sullivan. He replayed the conversation in his mind
and considered the consequences of his promise.
*She couldn't stay here by herself. He couldn't take her
with him to Texas. Where else could she go? She told him
she had no other relatives.*

For a long time, he lay there staring up at the roof
above him. His mind whirled, wrestling with the problem.

He didn't sleep much that night and rose before
daylight. A cold rain greeted him as he stepped from the
barn. He washed quickly beside the watering trough and
set in doing the morning chores. By the time he finished
the chores, smoke was rising from the chimney—Opal
was up.

He carried the bucket of milk to the house and
knocked before going inside, brushing the rain from his

clothes. The smell of fried salt pork greeted him. Opal was frying eggs. She twisted a worried look as he entered.

"What's wrong?" he asked.

"It's Pa. He's burning up with fever this morning. He looks bad."

"I know. I noticed it when we talked yesterday," he said, setting the bucket of milk on the work table.

"What can we do?" she asked, fear evident in her voice.

"I'll go take a look at him."

J. C. walked to Mr. Sullivan's room and opened the door quietly. He lay in bed with his eyes closed. J. C. reached a hand and touched the forehead. Opal was right; the man was burning up with fever and his breathing was ragged. He turned and quickly left the room.

"We've got to get his fever down," he told Opal. "Get a rag and bathe his face."

She poured water into a pan and hurried to do as he suggested. Anxious minutes turned into hours. Daylight was lost in darkness. Still, the fever persisted. J. C. left the room to see to the chores.

Sometime just before daylight, Mr. Sullivan gasped his final breath and died. Opal was holding his hand when the time came. J. C. slowly pulled the cover over her father's face and held her until the weeping subsided.

They buried Mr. Sullivan the following day beside his late wife on a swell of ground behind the cabin.

CHAPTER VI

The cold days of winter passed slowly. Each day after the evening chores were done, he spent at least an hour practicing throwing his heavy hunting knife. He had progressed to the point he could pin a falling leaf to the tree from which it fell.

Opal begged J. C. to move into the house and use her pa's bedroom, but he steadfastly refused. He continued to sleep in the hayloft of the barn.

J. C. spent every spare minute repairing the old wagon. He managed to replace two broken spokes, rebuild the sides, and strengthen the axle.

"Why are you working so hard fixing up that old wagon?" Opal asked over breakfast one morning.

"Come spring, we need to leave here. I figured traveling would be easier in a wagon."

"Leave? Where we going?"

"Texas. We can't stay here."

"Why not?" she questioned.

"We just can't, that's all. It ain't right us living here together."

"What's wrong with it? We ain't done nothing wrong. I thought you liked it here."

"I do, but it just ain't right, that's all. We're leaving, come spring. That's my final word on the matter."

J. C.'s days were filled with work around the cabin and hunting to provide meat for their needs. Opal cooked their meals and kept the cabin clean and orderly. Nothing more was said on the subject of them leaving. He continued sleeping in the barn.

Gradually, winter spent itself and the days grew warmer. J. C. knew it was almost time to leave.

"Start gathering up what you want to take with us," he told her at breakfast. "We'll load it in the wagon. I figure on leaving day after tomorrow."

"I ain't going!" she told him flat out.

He jerked a surprised look up at her.

"I promised your pa I'd take care of you and that's what I'm gonna do. We're leaving day after tomorrow and that's all there is to it."

"You can't make me go!"

"Well, you sure can't stay here. I won't leave you here. I promised your pa."

"You don't want me to go with you to Texas. I'm not going where I'm not wanted!"

"Opal, it ain't that I don't want you to go, I do. I just don't know what else to do. I promised your pa and I ain't gonna go back on my word."

Silence settled between them for a long spell. Finally, she nodded her head.

"I'll start gathering stuff together."

"Get up, Tom!" J. C. hollered, as he popped the long reins against the mule's rump.

The big, brown Missouri mule leaned into the horse collar and their wagon moved forward.

Opal sat on the small, board seat beside him. She sat upright with her head held high and her gaze straight ahead. Only once did he see her twist a look backwards toward the only home she had ever known—where both of her parents were buried.

A sad expression flashed across her face for only an instant before she turned her face back toward the road ahead with a look of determination he had never seen before.

It was a crisp, spring morning. A faint hint of pink tinted the eastern horizon.

Behind their wagon, Blackie and the milk cow followed on short lead lines. On the floor underneath the seat, his four Kentucky long rifles lay, loaded and ready in case they encountered trouble.

Opal's worldly belongings, as well as their bedding, were contained in a wooden chest he had made specifically for that purpose.

After traveling an hour or so, they came upon a road leading toward the southwest and followed it until they encountered a large river. The road turned upriver for a mile or so until it crossed the river at a shallow crossing.

By nightfall, J. C. figured they had traveled twenty miles or so. He found a small, fresh-running creek and pulled to a stop.

"We'll make camp here for the night," he told Opal. "I'll get a fire started and then tend the stock while you fix us some supper."

Opal nodded agreement and jumped down from the wagon.

He gathered small sticks and firewood and had a fire going in no time. He led their mule, horse, and milk cow to the creek for water. While the animals drank thirstily, he swung a look around.

It was a good camping spot. Far enough off the road not to be disturbed by any passer-by, with good water and green grass for the stock. Tall sycamore and giant oak trees with their limbs spread out in a forty foot circle gave witness of the fertile land.

Over by the fire, Opal was busy preparing supper. Her attitude had changed during their long ride that day. She looked happier than he had seen her in several days. She was a good girl. No, as he looked closer at her, he had to admit she was no longer a girl, but a full growed *woman.*

Suddenly embarrassed by his thoughts, he jerked his gaze away. Blackie, Ole Tom, and the milk cow had slaked their thirst. He led them to a patch of green grass near the campsite and hobbled them.

"Coffee's ready," Opal said, slicing salt pork into the frying pan. "Supper won't be long."

"No hurry," he told her, taking a tin cup and pouring it full from the blackened coffee pot. "We ain't in no hurry to get anywhere anyhow."

He sat on the ground near the fire.

"Hello, the camp!" a high-pitched man's voice called out from the gathering darkness.

J. C. snatched up one of the Kentucky long rifles lying nearby. He raked back the striker.

"Who are you and what you want?" he called loudly.

"Passing by and smelled your coffee."

"Come on in with your hands empty," he called.

A bearded old fellow appeared from the darkness leading a grey mule and stepped into the circle of light from the campfire. It was hard to judge his age, but he moved nimbly as he led his saddled horse into camp.

J. C. looked the old-timer over with a searching look. At first glance, he saw no threat; the ancient flintlock rifle he carried looked like it would blow up if it were fired. He wore fringed, deerskin clothes much like J. C.'s. A tomahawk and large hunting knife protruded from under his wide, leather belt.

"Wondering if you could spare a cup?"

"Don't see why not," he told the old fellow. "Come on in and sit."

"Mighty neighborly of ye," he said, pulling a square of tobacco from his pocket and slicing off a large plug. "If'n that coffee tastes half as good as it smells, it'll be like heaven on earth."

Opal filled a tin cup and handed it to the man. He took it and parted his grey beard with a wide smile.

"Much obliged, ma'am. Where you young folks be headed?"

"Texas," J. C. told him.

The old timer jerked a surprised look over the rim of his coffee cup at the answer.

"Mighty long trail to Texas. Got any notion where you are right now?"

"No, does it matter?" J. C. asked.

"It matters. 'Cause you're in what's called the *Un-organized Territory*. It's the home of savage Indians and they don't take kindly to visitors. They'll lift your scalps and hang them on their lodge pole before you get a day's ride."

"Why? We ain't bothering nobody."

"They don't need a reason. You're a white man intruding on their land, that's all the reason they need. The way they see it, it's no different than if you come into their teepee without being invited."

"I ain't never seen no *savage Indian*," J. C. told him. "Just some back at Fort Gibson that seemed tame to me."

"Sonny, if you see one, it's done too late."

"I think you're joshin' me."

Before answering, the old timer spat a stream of tobacco juice into the campfire.

"I'm serious as a rifle ball between the eyes. If you're headed for Texas, you should'a swung south through Louisiana. Your chances of getting to Texas going this way is about like a snowball in Hades."

"I didn't know. If it's as bad as you say, what you doin' here?"

The old timer cackled a high-pitched belly laugh. "I been fightin' them redskins since I was knee-high to a jack rabbit. They all know old *Jubal Tucker!* More'n a few have tried to lift my scalp and died trying. That's their scalps hanging from my saddle yonder."

J. C. swung a look. He saw what looked like two dozen or more long, black locks of human hair clinging to dried skin and hanging from the old timer's saddle.

"Why do you carry them around?"

"Indians are a superstitious lot. They put a heap of stock in how many scalps they can hang on their lodge pole. Them scalps yonder are a powerful warning to others giving thought about trying to lift this old grey scalp of mine."

"So you've killed lots of men?" J. C. asked.

"I never killed a man that wasn't trying to kill me."

"Supper's almost ready. Would you eat with us, Mr. Tucker?" Opal asked.

"Well, now, I can't remember ever turning down an invite for supper from a pretty lady."

The old-timer sat cross-legged beside the campfire and devoured two plates of fried potatoes and salt pork like a starving wolf. When he finished, he licked the grease from his fingers as he spoke.

"You youngin's seem to me like a good sort. I got no place I gotta be until I take a notion to get there. If you got no objections, I'll jest mosey along with you and keep the Indians shooed away."

"We'd be mighty obliged, Mr. Tucker," J. C. told him. "I'm green as a sour persimmon about this sort of thing."

"You'll learn, son . . . if you live long enough."

"I'd be obliged for anything you could teach me."

"We'll see," the old-timer said over the rim of his coffee cup. "We'll see. Ma'am, you shore perk up a mighty fine coffee."

"Thank you, Mr. Tucker."

"Now lookie here! If we're gonna travel together, call me *Jubal*. Mr. Tucker was my pa, and he's been dead and gone more years than I care to remember."

"I couldn't help noticing that old flintlock rifle you carry," J. C. said. "Does it still shoot?"

"Yep, now and then, anyway. It's come near getting me killed a time or two. It gets contrary about shooting from time to time."

J. C. rose and walked over to the wagon. He lifted one of the Kentucky long rifles he took from the highwaymen back in Tennessee and pitched it to Jubal.

"Here, maybe this one will work better. Be careful, it's loaded."

Jubal deftly caught the rifle in mid-air. He looked it over closely, gently caressing it with his hand from end to end. He lifted it to his shoulder and sighted along the barrel.

"Seen 'em before, but never been able to scrape together the where-withal to get myself one. That's a mighty-fine piece of hardware."

"It's yours."

Jubal Tucker jerked a surprised look. His whiskers parted and a wide smile flashed across his lips.

"Lived a long time," he said. "Nobody never give me nothing 'cept a hard time. I'm beholden to you, son."

"Name's J. C. Holderfield. This here is Opal Sullivan."

"Figured she was your woman."

"No, her pa died a ways back. Before he died, I promised him I'd take care of her. That's what I mean to do."

"Mighty decent of you," Jubal said, swallowing the last of his coffee.

"Reckon we best try to get some shuteye before our company decides to pay us a visit."

"What you mean, *company?*" J. C. asked, confusion clouding his face. "You mean the *Indians?*"

"Yep, they been watching us for a spell now."

J. C. snatched up the rifle that lay within easy reach. His head twisted this way and that, searching for a sign of the Indians.

"Easy, boy. Don't go getting nervous jest yet. They'll wait until we get bedded down. Besides, like I said before, you ain't gonna see 'em until they want you to see 'em; by then, it's too late."

"Then how do you know they're watching us?"

"Ever smell a polecat?"

"Yeah, of course, lots of them. Why?"

"Can you recall what they smell like?"

"Of course. How could anybody forget that smell?"

"Well, Indians are jest like that. Ain't nothing else in the world smells like a wild Indian. They smell of smoke, spoiled grease, and the wild game they eat. Sort of a wild, pungent smell. Jest like the polecat, once you smell a Indian, you won't never forget it."

"Are you saying you can smell them right now?"

"Yep."

"Then shouldn't we get ready?"

"We will. Be patient, son. Indians don't git in no hurry. They can lay still as a dead log for hours at a time without so much as a deep breath. They talk to one another mockin' the night sounds, like a bird or coyote. Like I said, they won't come until we get bedded down."

"How will we know when they're fixing to attack?" J. C. asked.

"We won't. But we'll be ready and then it won't matter. Take your knife and cut some small limbs. We'll mound 'em up under our blankets to look like we're sleeping, but we'll be over yonder in them bushes waitin'."

J. C. did as his new friend suggested. He cut small limbs from the nearby bushes and bunched them underneath their blankets. He even placed his coonskin cap at the head of his bedroll like he still had it on his head.

When all was ready, J. C. and Opal took up a loaded rifle and headed for the nearby bushes.

"Where you gonna be?" J. C. asked.

"I'll be in the woods. Maybe I can find some of them before they have a chance to come for us."

J. C. blinked his eyes and the old-timer was gone—one second he was standing there—the next he was nowhere in sight—like a ghost. J. C. was amazed how the man could move so quickly without making a sound.

A giant, dead log with bushes growing along its length offered a clear view of their campsite and some measure of protection. Opal lay down near one end of the log and he took the other end. Now all they could do was wait.

It was a beautiful, early spring evening. A jillion stars winked at them from a coal-black canopy overhead. A thin slice of moon offered sparse light.

Night sounds drifted on a slight breeze and somewhere, a whippoorwill called to its mate—or was it *really* a whippoorwill? Maybe it was the Indians talking to one another like Jubal said they did.

Nervous sweat from his hands wet the stock of the Kentucky long rifle he gripped. He checked the extra one laying beside him to make sure it was loaded and ready. He flicked a glance at Opal. She was looking at him nervously. He offered a slight nod of encouragement.

How long did they wait? He had no idea. Minutes stretched into what seemed like an eternity. The campfire burned itself into nothing more than small, flickering flames—still they waited and watched.

It sounded like nothing more than several night birds in flight—except *these* birds were small feathers attached to the end of long, deadly arrows. J. C. heard the soft *swishing* sound, followed by the thud when the deadly points buried themselves into their blankets.

A heartbeat after the arrows struck, three dark-skinned Indians burst from the darkness into the faint light from the campfire. Their faces were streaked with wavy lines of paint. Each of them carried a tomahawk or war club. They rushed toward the blankets for a final, killing blow, screaming as they ran.

"Now!" J. C. called out to Opal.

Two explosions shattered the night almost as one. The heavy, lead balls from their Kentucky long rifles, fired from point-blank range, buried deep into the chests of two of the warriors. The force of the slugs halted their charge and they tumbled to the ground.

The third warrior hesitated for only an instant and twisted a surprised look toward their location. Raising his war club above his head, he let out a blood-curdling scream and charged directly toward them. J. C. instinctively knew there wasn't time to grab up his extra rifle, pull back the striker, and still have time to kill his attacker.

He snatched his hunting knife from its belt scabbard and flung it in one smooth motion with all his might. The big knife twisted end over end in its flight and buried deep in the Indian's chest. The man stumbled. His legs buckled beneath him, but his forward momentum landed him on top of J. C.

J. C. gasped for air and flung the Indian off him, but the smell of his attacker lodged in his memory—Jubal was right—he would never forget the smell.

"You fought good, pilgrim!" Jubal cackled, as he emerged from the edge of darkness carrying three bloody scalps in one hand and his wide-bladed hunting knife in the other.

"That was the last of 'em. I got these three before the attack," he said, lifting the bloody scalps high.

The sight sickened J. C., and he could only imagine what it did to Opal. He twisted a look at her. She was on her hands and knees, emptying her stomach.

"Want me to show you how to peel the scalp off the other three?"

J. C. swallowed back the bile that threatened to erupt and shook his head.

CHAPTER VII

They fought off two more Indian attacks during the next month's journey. In the process, Jubal collected five more scalps to add to his collection and displayed them proudly from his saddle.

"Them wild savages look us over most every day," Jubal told them. "They see my string of scalps and most decide we ain't worth the risk. Them scalps save us lots of fights."

The long days with the grizzled, old woodsman proved to be invaluable. J. C. learned the art of tracking and hunting both animals and humans. He learned how to live off the land. He learned which plants were good to eat and which were poisonous. He learned which could be used to doctor certain illnesses. Perhaps the most important thing he learned was how to kill without remorse.

"When a man's trying to kill you, you only got two choices. You can die or kill him before he kills you. I never cottoned to the first choice. You're a good man, J. C., and I got a notion you'll go far."

Opal responded quickly to life on the trail. She assumed the role of setting up camp at each stop and provided a fresh pot of coffee and a meal within minutes. J. C. also discovered that she was a crack shot with the long rifle.

Jubal and Opal grew closer with each passing day. He treated her like a daughter. J. C. still looked at her more like the sister he never had.

"We'll cross the Red River into the Republic of Texas tomorrow," Jubal informed them at supper one evening. "I hear tell they got Indian troubles there too, so I'll stay with you a few more weeks until we find a safe spot."

"You could just stay with us," Opal said.

"I never been much at putting down roots," Jubal said. "I'm kinda like the wind. Free to wander wherever I take a notion."

"That's the way I am, too," J. C. said, returning Opal's look. She quickly looked away.

True to his word, they struck the Red River just before sundown the following day. They made camp on the near bank.

"We'll cross come morning when it's light," Jubal told them as they sipped coffee around the campfire. "Don't want to get caught in the river when it gets dark, in case we have trouble."

"What kind of trouble?" J. C. wanted to know.

"I hear tell the Red is a sandy-bottom river. If we ain't careful, it can swallow up our wagon before we know it, especially this time of year. The rain up river's got it running bank to bank."

"What are we gonna do?" Opal asked.

"We'll cut us a couple of big logs and lash them to the wheels on both sides of the wagon. Then we'll tie ropes to the wagon and use the mule to float it across."

"Never would have thought of that," J. C. told him.

They moved the wagon to the shallow part of the water and lashed the big logs below the hub of the wheels. They swam J. C.'s horse and the two mules across the river, holding onto their tails and carrying the loose end of two long ropes.

The river was close to a hundred yards wide at the crossing. They reached the far side and climbed from the muddy water.

"Hook one of the mules to each of the ropes," Jubal instructed.

After the mules were hooked up, Jubal and J. C. each took hold of the bridle of a mule.

"Ready?" Jubal shouted.

"Ready!" J. C. answered.

They led both mules forward. The ropes tightened and the wagon moved forward into deeper water.

"It's floating!" Opal shouted excitedly.

When the wagon reached the current of the river, it swung sideways. The swift-running current carried it downstream.

"Pull faster!" Jubal shouted.

J. C. tugged on Ole Tom's bridle. The big mules leaned into their harnesses. Their hooves dug deep. The mules strained. Their leg muscles bulged. J. C. tugged on the bridle, almost running to keep up with the pace of the mules.

"It's halfway across!" Opal shouted at the top of her voice.

"Hee-yaw!" J. C. hollered at his mule, urging him to even greater effort.

J. C. dared not look back. He kept his gaze fixed straight ahead, tugging hard at the mule's bridle.

"It's across!" Opal screamed excitedly. "It's touched the bank downstream!"

"Whoa, big mule," J. C. said, patting the mule's nose.

"Tie the extra rope I gave you to the front of the wagon and to a tree while we hold it where it is," Jubal hollered.

The girl hurried to do as Jubal instructed. In short order, she had the wagon secured.

"Now we'll let off the ropes and hook the mules back up to the wagon," Jubal said.

After the mules were hitched up to the wagon, they used their hunting knives to cut the logs loose from the wheels and pushed them free.

Two days later, they encountered a traveler who identified the creek they were about to cross as Keechi Creek and the nearby *settlement* as *Mesquieteville.*

The settlement turned out to consist entirely of a single, log trading post.

"We best restock our supplies," J. C. suggested.

Opal pulled their wagon to a stop in front of the trading post as J. C. and Jubal slid from the mounts and tied them to the hitching post. A bearded old fellow sitting on a bench in front of the trading post looked up from his whittling and eyed them with interest.

"Howdy," the whittler greeted. "You folks traveling or going somewheres?"

"Traveling," Jubal said, spitting a long stream of brown tobacco juice into the dust. "Looking fer Texas."

"You found it. You been in Texas since you crossed the big river. We become part of the Union of the United States jest last December."

"You don't say! Well, what you know about that?" Jubal said, swiping the coonskin cap from his head and beating the dust from it against his leg.

"We're still having a passel of trouble with Mexico, though. They're still claiming Texas is part of Mexico. There's a lot of talk about war."

"Don't know nothing 'bout that," Jubal told him. "I'm mostly a loner myself. Don't spend a lot of time with other folks."

"How far to the next town?" J. C. asked.

"Town? The only *towns* that I heard anything 'bout in Texas is San Antonio and Nacogdoches. It's a long way to either one. Fact is, it's a long way to anywhere in Texas. But the way folks are flocking in, towns'll be springing up all over the place."

"Is the storekeeper inside?" J. C. asked.

"She shore is," the whittler said.

J. C. and Opal walked through the open door into the trading post. A middle age woman with a dingy-colored apron greeted them with a wide smile.

"Morning, young folks!" the woman greeted cheerfully. "How can I help you?"

"We need a few supplies," J. C. told her.

"Pick out whatever we need," he said, twisting a look at Opal.

The girl nodded.

"We could use a slab of salt pork and a peck of potatoes, if you have them."

"We got the salt pork, but we're out of potatoes. Got some good turnips, though."

"They'll do. We need a sack of salt and some of them dried apples there," she said, pointing to a small, open keg.

The store lady gathered the supplies and laid them on the counter.

"Anything else?"

"Don't reckon," Opal told her.

J. C. paid the lady for their supplies and carried them out to the wagon. Jubal was still jawin' with the old whittler.

"What'd the old-timer have to say?" J. C. asked Jubal.

"He said to keep a sharp eye out for Indians."

"Thought we'd be over and done with Indian troubles once we got in Texas."

"Guess not," Jubal said, shrugging his shoulders."

They camped that night beside a river that the old whittler had identified to Jubal as the west fork of the Trinity.

The country had flattened out. A man on horseback could see for miles in every direction. He stepped to the ground and sifted a handful of dirt through his fingers. The land was fertile.

This ground would grow anything a man had a mind to plant in it, J. C. thought. But he had no thought of being a farmer—he had his can-full of that life already.

"Where you got in mind to settle?" Jubal asked over the rim of his coffee cup as they sat around a small campfire after supper.

"Don't know," J. C. answered honestly. "First place I come to where I can find a job, I reckon."

"Been kinda thinkin' 'bout headin' on back. This here country don't feel like home."

"Hate to see you go, but understand how you feel," J. C. told him.

"Why don't you just stay with us, Jubal?" Opal asked. "We're kinda like *family* already."

"Like to, child, but a man's gotta do what a man's gotta do."

"When you leaving?" J. C. asked.

"Be headin' back come first light."

"We'll miss you," he told the old timer. "I'm much obliged for all you taught me."

"Put it to good use. It might help save your hair."

Jubal mounted his grey mule and rode out before good light. J. C. and Opal stood side by side and watched him go.

"Wish he had stayed with us," Opal said sadly. "Reckon we'll ever see him again?"

"It's a mighty big country, but you never know who's gonna cross your trail."

They broke camp before sunup and continued south. Deep arroyos separated rolling hills as they traveled, causing frequent detours. Just before mid-afternoon, gunshots echoed among the hills and reached their hearing.

J. C. motioned Opal to rein up and remain where she was while he checked out the shooting. He loaded one of the extra Kentucky long rifles and tied it underneath the fender of his saddle. Taking up a second one, he rode out.

From the sound of the shooting, he determined it was coming from just beyond a large hill up ahead. Before reaching the top, he reined up and tied Blackie to a bush and proceeded on foot.

He bellied down and crawled the last few yards to the crest of the hill. He found a large rock surrounded by low-growing bushes and looked down.

Four men were pinned down in a shallow gully, surrounded and outnumbered by a dozen or more uniformed Mexicans. The Mexicans were pouring hot lead into the gully, keeping the Americans pinned down. What little return fire there was coming from the Americans was a different-sounding shot, not nearly as loud as the Mexican rifles. Several dead horses lay in and around the gully where the men had taken cover. A large herd of horses was being tended by a uniformed Mexican behind the protection of a nearby hill.

From his location at the top of the hill, J. C. could look down on the Mexicans' position. Without help, the Americans were done for. He decided to even up the odds.

He braced the long barrel of his rifle against the rock, lined up the sight on the chest of one of the Mexican soldiers, and feathered the trigger.

The rifle bucked against his shoulder. He watched as the soldier's body jumped from the impact of the rifle ball before tumbling to the ground. He laid the empty rifle down and snatched up his second. He jammed it to his shoulder and fired again—another soldier tumbled over.

The remaining soldiers returned fire and scrambled to find cover as J. C. quickly reloaded both rifles. Rifle balls ricocheted off the rock in front of him and sailed harmlessly into the air. Again and again and again he reloaded and fired. Finally, seeing many of their fellow comrades struck down, the rest fled to their horses, quickly mounted, and rode away at a gallop.

Slowly, cautiously, the four Americans emerged from the protection of their gully. J. C. stood and walked slowly down the hill to meet them.

The first to emerge was a slight-built man with long, dark hair and an almost feminine face, but the authority in his dark, penetrating eyes identified him as an obvious leader of men. He wore a metal star pinned to his coat. He approached J. C. with an appreciative look and a hand extended.

"I'm Captain Samuel Walker with the Texas Rangers."

J. C. set the butt of both of his loaded Kentucky long rifles against the ground and held them with his left hand. He took the man's right hand with his own in a firm handshake.

"I'm J. C. Holderfield."

"You saved our bacon, Mr. Holderfield. We're obliged. We run out of ammunition for our rifles and was left with nothing except our pistols. They were of little value against the Mexicans' rifles."

"Glad to be of help."

Three other men emerged from the gully; one of them was wounded in the leg. J. C. saw two others lying in the gully—dead.

"Where you from, Mr. Holderfield?"

"Tennessee."

"What brings you to this part of Texas?"

"Looking for work. I've got a young lady with me. She's in our wagon over the hill yonder."

"What kind of work you looking for?"

"Anything to earn bean wages."

"I'll need to see to my wounded and bury my dead. We were headed to Sod Horton's ranch a few miles to the east when we run into the Mexicans. If you'd want to get your wagon and join us, I might have a proposal for you."

"I'll go and fetch my wagon."

Opal pulled the wagon to a stop. The wounded Ranger was cared for and loaded into the wagon. J. C. led the way on Blackie, followed by the wagon. Capt. Walker and his fellow Rangers walked behind.

Darkness overtook them and they made camp beside a fresh-running stream. One of the Rangers built a fire and Opal made coffee and started supper. After J. C. saw to the animals, he poured himself a cup of coffee and squatted beside the fire with the others.

"If you hadn't come along when you did, we were done for," Capt. Walker told him. "We're indebted to you for saving our lives."

"I just done what anybody else would have done," J. C. said, sipping his coffee.

"No, few men would have taken up the fight at the risk of their own safety. Nonetheless, I'm indebted to you—a debt I could never repay. Know anything about the Texas Rangers?"

"Never heard of them until now."

"We're a law enforcement agency with state-wide jurisdiction. We're charged with keeping the peace and enforcing the laws of Texas. Our jurisdiction covers 268,000 square acres.

"I'm presently forming my own company under the command of General Zachary Taylor. Do you think you might be interested in becoming a Texas Ranger?"

"You mean a *lawman?*" J. C. asked, surprised at the question. "Never thought about becoming a lawman."

"From what I seen back there, you got a lot of sand in you. I think you'd make a good Ranger."

"I reckon I don't know what you mean."

"It means you ain't afraid of a fight."

"Oh, I swore an oath to Miss Opal's dying father that I would look after her," J. C. explained. "I could never go back on my word."

They dropped the subject.

The Horton Ranch was the biggest J. C. had ever seen. A huge, log fort-like stockade with guard towers surrounded the main house.

He counted six large barns in a long line with split-rail corrals connecting them all. A fresh-running creek ran along the bottom of the hill in front of the complex. A large herd of horses grazed along the creek bed. Several herds of Longhorn cattle grazed along the hillside, watched over by several cowboys. Both J. C. and Opal marveled at the place.

As they drove through the open, double gate into a large yard, a middle-aged couple emerged from a sprawling log house.

Opal pulled Ole Tom to a stop. J. C. reined down and sat his saddle as Capt. Walker hurried to meet the couple.

The ranch owner was a big man who towered over all the others nearby. He was broad-shouldered with a narrow waist. His face was tanned the color of old saddle leather. His long, grey hair hung below his shirt collar. A matching handle-bar mustache covered his top lip.

The woman beside him had a happy smile on her pretty face. Her dark hair was gathered into a bun on top of her head, and she wore a long work dress that touched the top of her shoes.

"Howdy, Sod," Walker greeted.

"Captain," the man replied, extending a welcoming hand.

Capt. Walker took the offered hand and they shook hands like family.

"We ran into some trouble back a ways. Lost two good men and got another wounded in the wagon."

The rancher turned a look to a Mexican woman nearby.

"See to the wounded man," he ordered, with a voice that commanded authority.

Two Mexican men hurried forward to help the wounded Ranger from the wagon. The Mexican woman ushered them into a nearby building.

"This here is J. C. Holderfield and Opal Sullivan," Capt. Walker said. "This young fellow came along at the right time and saved our bacon. Two dozen Mexican soldiers had us surrounded and out of ammunition. We were goners for sure. He killed several of them and the rest lit a shuck."

The big rancher walked the few steps to stand beside J. C.'s horse. He lifted a hand.

J. C. grasped the rancher's work-hardened hand in a firm handshake.

"Known Sam a long time," the rancher said. "He's a good man. Shore would hate to lose him. I'm obliged to you. You and Miss Sullivan are welcome here."

"Thanks, Mr. Horton."

"That's quite a gelding you're riding there, Mr. Holderfield. Don't reckon you'd be interested in selling him?"

"No, sir."

"Figured as much, but never hurts to ask. I'm always looking for good horse flesh."

"You folks come on into the house and sit a spell," Mrs. Horton welcomed. "Coffee's hot."

They were ushered into the biggest house J. C. had ever seen. The spacious den had two cowhide sofas, one on either side of a ceiling-high, rock fireplace. The sofas were separated by a colorful Mexican woven rug. A large deer head was mounted on each side of the fireplace. Both J. C. and Opal stared in amazement.

A Mexican lady poured coffee for everyone as they were seated.

"How's the recruiting coming along, Sam?" the rancher asked.

"Well, losing two of my Rangers yesterday set me back some, but I'll have my company formed and ready to ride when the time comes we're needed."

"Sounds like that won't be long off if the Mexican army is ranging this far from the border."

"Gen. Taylor is moving his army into San Antonio," Walker said. "War's coming, no doubt about it; I'm guessing we'll be at war with Mexico in less than a month."

"That soon, huh?"

"That's what I'm figuring."

All the talk of war was news to J. C. They visited the day away. After a delicious supper, Mrs. Horton took Opal to show her the bedroom where she would be spending the night.

Mr. Horton and the captain went outside to enjoy a smoke. J. C. excused himself and went to the barn to check on Blackie and Ole Tom. He returned to find the rancher and Ranger captain talking serious like.

"I talked to Sod about Miss Sullivan staying here on the ranch," Capt. Walker told J. C.

"He said they would be happy to have her stay."

"Matter of fact, it would be good for Evelyn for the girl to be here," Mr. Horton added. "We've never been able to have children, and she'd be a lot of company for the wife."

"That would be mighty decent of you folks, Mr. Horton," J. C. said. "I'll talk to Opal and see how she feels about it."

"Yes—yes, you do that," Capt. Walker said. "Sod has agreed to provide horses for my men. We'll be riding out at first light. We'd be glad to have you join up as a Ranger."

"I'll let you know in short order," J. C. promised.

He excused himself and went looking for Opal. He found her and Mrs. Horton sitting in the den, talking excitedly, laughing, and sipping coffee.

"Hello, J. C.," Mrs. Horton greeted. "Pour yourself a cup and join us. Opal was just telling me about how you got your wagon across the Red River. It sounds exciting."

"Yes, ma'am, it was—and a little scary, too."

"We've had the best time visiting," Opal told him.

"That's good. Could you and me go for a little walk?" he asked.

A serious look swept across her face. She flicked glances between him and Mrs. Horton before nodding her head and rising.

"Would you excuse us?" she asked politely.

"Of course," the rancher's wife said, smiling.

They left the sprawling ranch house and strolled slowly toward the barn where Blackie and Ole Tom were stalled. He struggled in his mind how to approach the subject of her remaining with the Hortons. The long quietness bred anxiousness, which turned quickly into tenseness.

He suddenly stopped, reached out his hands and took her hands in his. He looked deep into her questioning eyes.

"Opal, there's something we need to talk about."

A worried look clouded her pretty face. The look hurt his heart. For the first time since he met her, he *really* looked at her closely and was shocked at just how pretty she was and what his heart was telling him about how he honestly felt about her.

"What is it, J. C.? What's wrong?"

"With all the scrapes we've had with the Indians, we've been mighty lucky. Fact is, if it hadn't been for Jubal, both of us would have been dead a long ways back up the trail. Now, they tell me the Indians here in Texas are just as bad, if not worse.

"On top of that, they're saying a war between Texas and Mexico is about to break out. Mr. and Mrs. Horton have invited you to stay here with them. They'd take good care of you and you'd be safe here."

Opal's eyes got big. Her lips started to quiver.

"What are you gonna do? Where you going?" she asked in a quivering voice. "I want to go with you!" she pleaded.

He closed his eyes and shook his head.

"You can't go with me. Capt. Walker asked me to join up with the Texas Rangers. We'll be riding no telling where and most likely fighting. You need to stay here where you'll be safe."

"But—but if you go—I'll never see you again!"

"Yeah, you will. After I make something of myself, I'll come back and get you."

"You promise?" she asked through choking sobs.

"I promise!" he said, loosing her hands and wrapping his strong arms around her. He pulled her to him. His trembling lips found hers. For the very first time—they kissed—a kiss that sealed a promise that would last a lifetime.

CHAPTER VIII

The dim grayness of a new day was quickly swallowing the darkness. A rosy dawn was breaking over the eastern horizon.

J. C. toed a stirrup and swung his leg over the saddle. He hefted his Kentucky long rifle in his left hand; his spare was tied securely beneath the right fender of his saddle. Beside him, Capt. Walker and the other two Rangers also stepped into their saddles.

J. C. sneaked a look. Sod Horton stood with his wife and Opal. Mrs. Horton had an arm wrapped around the girl's shoulders.

Opal had never looked as pretty as she did at that moment. He lifted his right hand into the air in a final *goodbye*. From his wrist, the ends of a yellow ribbon fluttered in the breeze—Opal's favorite ribbon.

She lifted her hand into the air.

"I'll be waiting for you!" she shouted.

Heels were jammed into their horses' flanks. The high-spirited mounts responded and the riders quickly disappeared in a cloud of dust. Capt. Walker led the way on a high-spirited, bay gelding. J. C. rode directly behind him on Blackie. Clete Gibbons and Jake Sawyer brought up the rear.

Capt. Walker set out in a steady short-lope and held the pace for three or four miles. Each man rode with his rifle across his saddle and his head constantly twisting back and forth, searching for any sign of trouble.

By sundown, J. C. figured they had easily covered forty miles. Capt. Walker still hadn't shared their destination.

Dusky-dark found them crossing a narrow creek where they reined up.

"We'll make camp for the night," Walker said, swinging to the ground.

Camp was quickly set up, a fire built, and water for creek coffee was set over the fire.

J. C. helped water the horses and put them on a picket line tied between two nearby trees.

Supper consisted of beef jerky and coffee. The four Rangers sat around the campfire sipping coffee and staring into the flames, each lost in his own thoughts. His last memory of Opal flashed from his memory. The mental picture warmed him inside.

Yes, he admitted for the first time, *I love her!*

His thoughts were scattered when Capt. Walker rose, walked to his saddlebags, and withdrew a pistol, ammunition, and a badge. He returned and handed the badge to J. C.

"Pin it on, raise your right hand, and repeat after me."

"I, J. C. Holderfield . . ."

"I, J. C. Holderfield."

"Do solemnly swear . . ."

"Do solemnly swear."

"To uphold and enforce the laws of the State of Texas . . ."

"To uphold and enforce the laws of the State of Texas."

"To the best of my ability . . ."

"To the best of my ability."

"So help me God!"

"So help me God."

"Congratulations, J. C. You are now a Texas Ranger. Here, this is a holster model Paterson revolver. The cylinder holds five, .36 caliber percussion loads and will fire as fast as you can thumb back the hammer and pull the trigger."

"I don't see a trigger," J. C. said, with a confused look.

The captain thumbed back the hammer. As he did, the trigger swung down from the belly of the weapon and locked in place.

"That prevents an accidental firing. I contend a thin strip of metal surrounding the trigger would accomplish the same thing with fewer complications. Someday I'll recommend my idea to Samuel Colt.

"Nonetheless, right now this is the best side-arm weapon we have available. Take it, it's yours."

J. C. gratefully accepted the weapon. He spent the next two hours examining the weapon. He disassembled it and put it back together again and again until he could accomplish it in the dark. From that moment forward, he practiced with both the pistol and his throwing knife at least an hour every night before retiring. Over and over—again and again—he drew the pistol from his waistband, aimed, and pretended to fire.

At times, they might travel days without encountering a single, living soul. Other times, they came across remote trading posts and small communities almost daily. At each one, Capt. Walker gathered every male between the ages of fourteen and forty to listen to his recruiting pitch. He ended each talk with an invitation to a "select few" to join up—occasionally a few did.

By the time they reached San Antonio, a full month later, Capt. Walker rode in front of a force of eighteen Rangers. A full two hours of each day was spent training the new recruits.

"Our motto will be, *One lawbreaker requires only one Texas Ranger to do the job!*" he told them. "*Any* order is to be obeyed *immediately* and *without question!*"

The country took on a drastic change. The thick, green forests turned to barren, rocky hills. Cactus and mesquite bushes replaced the green grass and bushes J. C. had grown used to. Small, muddy streams of water were the only water source for thirsty men and horses.

They rode in a column, two by two, with Capt. Walker in front. As they entered the sprawling town, he twisted his head to scan the column.

"Sit straight in your saddles, men; chests out, heads back, look proud! You're *TEXAS RANGERS—THE BEST LAWMEN IN TEXAS!*"

Townspeople paused on the streets and stared at the procession; others rushed from stores to see what was going on. An overwhelming feeling of pride swelled J. C.'s chest. For the first time in his life, he was part of something bigger than himself. *I'm a lawman . . . I'm actually a Texas Ranger!*

It seemed to J. C. that even Blackie somehow shared the same feeling. The coal-black gelding tossed his big head and seemed to lift his hooves a little higher than usual and pranced sideways.

The column of Rangers rode the length of the street and continued on out of town to a large Army encampment. It looked to J. C. like an endless sea of white tents in long rows. He had never seen that many men together in one place before. He guessed it was more than he could count.

Their tiny column reined up at a makeshift corral. Capt. Walker asked directions to the headquarters tent. A burly sergeant pointed directions.

"You men stay here. I'll ride over and report in," Capt. Walker instructed.

J. C. and the other Rangers dismounted, loosened cinch straps, and watered their mounts. When finished, they knelt in a circle near the corral and waited.

"You fellows the Texas Rangers we heard was coming?" a big, burly sergeant asked as he walked up. Three companions accompanied him.

"Reckon that's us," one of the Rangers, a fellow named Herb Dean, answered.

"Shore ain't what we expected. The way we heard it, you boys were supposed to be the toughest outfit in Texas. Guess we heard wrong."

"Guess so," Herb said, spitting a stream of tobacco juice and lifting a squinted look at the sergeant.

"Why don't you boys get back on your hosses and hightail it back where you come from? We don't need your help to whup a few Mex."

"Suits me," Herb said, shrugging his shoulders. "But we go where the captain says we go."

"I say you're all a bunch of cowards, that's what I say."

At those words, every Ranger stood to his feet and turned to face the four soldiers.

"Mister," Herb said through clenched teeth, "Nobody calls me a coward, nobody!"

"What's going on here?" Capt. Walker said, walking up and overhearing the last exchange.

"Who are you?" the sergeant demanded in a hard voice.

"I'm *Capt.* Samuel Walker. Commander of this Texas Ranger Company, attached to General Zachary Taylor's United States Army. I believe it's customary to salute a superior officer, is it not, *Sergeant?"*

The sergeant paused for only a moment before lifting a half-hearted salute. Captain Walker snapped a smart salute.

"You're excused, Sergeant."

The four soldiers turned and stalked away.

"The chow tent is down that way," Walker said, pointing. "You men go fill your bellies. Then find the quartermaster tent and check out two rations of ammunition each. We'll be riding in two hours."

The Rangers hurried to obey his orders without a question. They found the chow tent and were fed beef stew, cornpone, and coffee. After they had eaten their fill, they found the quartermaster tent and picked up their ammunition.

"Reckon where we're headed?" one of the Rangers asked no one in particular.

"Like Herb said awhile ago," J. C. said. "Wherever the Captain says we go."

In less than two hours, the Rangers were gathered back at the corral, with supplies loaded, girths cinched, and were waiting beside their horses when Capt. Walker rode up.

"Mount and form up, two by two's. We're riding."

Led by Capt. Walker, the Ranger Company rode south toward the disputed territory bordered by the Rio Grande River.

By the time they reached the river it was dusky-dark. Capt. Walker raised his right hand signaling a halt.

"We'll make dry camp over yonder in that willow thicket. Hide the horses—no fires."

After their mounts were cared for, they all sat in a circle, well hidden by the thick willows, and chewed on beef jerky and hard tack.

"Men, we've been assigned to conduct guerrilla warfare along the border. Our mission is to locate and scout out the enemy, try to determine their next move, and report back to headquarters. When possible, we are also ordered to disrupt and destroy their supply lines through ambush and hit and run attacks.

"One other thing. Except for the purpose of obtaining information from captured officers, we don't take prisoners. Officers can be important sources of information, so, given the opportunity, capture them alive. Is that clear?"

He paused and swept a slow look around the circle at each man. He waited for a nodded acknowledgment before proceeding.

"We don't have the time or means to take care of prisoners. If any man has a problem with that, you can fork your horse and ride out right now."

No one made a move.

"Alright then, get some sleep; we ride out before daylight."

CHAPTER IX

The following morning, the Rangers were separated in pairs and sent across the Rio Grande into Mexican territory. They took up positions in hiding approximately five miles inside Mexico and were told to watch for movement of the enemy.

J. C. and Herb Dean lay belly-down in a thick growth of low-lying bushes, watching a long column of Mexican soldiers moving toward the Rio Grande. All of the Mexicans were on foot except for a few officers.

As best they could, they counted to a hundred, made a mark in the sand, and started counting again. When the column had passed out of sight, they added the marks—thirty-four.

"We need to get this information back to the Captain right away," Herb said.

"Want me to go?" J. C. asked.

"No, I'll go. You stay here and keep watching, there might be more coming."

J. C. nodded and settled down to keep watch as Herb Dean pushed to his knees and made his way to where they had left their horses.

An hour passed and then another. He kept his gaze fixed on the sloping hill to his south. Suddenly, something moved! He stared harder. It was a single Mexican rider, most likely a scout. The rider moved cautiously to the crest of the hill, paused, and scanned the area ahead of him before moving closer to J. C.'s location.

J. C. eased his Kentucky long rifle up and sighted along the barrel.

Should I shoot him or let him pass? He wrestled with the question in his mind. His finger rested on the trigger as he tried to decide what to do.

If he's a scout, they've sent him on ahead for a reason; another army column maybe? Reckon I best wait and see what he's up to.

He hunkered back down into the bushes and allowed the rider to pass within forty yards.

He heard them before he saw them. A two-hitch team of mules crested the hill pulling a heavy cannon mounted on wheels. Four out-riders surrounded the piece of artillery.

The first was followed closely by another and then another. A total of four cannons rolled down the sloping hillside toward the river. The mules strained to move the heavy loads through the sandy ground. The out-riders lashed out with long whips. Behind the cannons, he counted two hundred mounted soldiers.

Finally, all four cannons and the mounted cavalry passed his location and disappeared from sight. He watched and waited, thinking maybe another group might appear.

I need to let the Captain know about the cannons and cavalry, J. C. decided. He was about to slip from his hiding place when riders suddenly crested the hill. He hunkered back down and watched.

Two Mexican army officers, with two guards riding on either side of them, rode slowly down the sloping hillside directly toward his hiding place. Although he wasn't familiar with the marks of rank on their shoulders, he could tell they were important officers of high authority.

What was it Capt. Walker had said about capturing Mexican officers? Oh yeah, he said they could be an important source of information. Should I try to capture these officers?

J. C. slipped the Paterson pistol from his belt and thumbed back the hammer. He carefully laid it on the sand in front of him. Next, he checked the load in his Kentucky rifle again, just to make sure. He thumbed back the striker and sighted along the barrel. His hands made sweat on the wooden stock as he waited.

The little procession rode closer and closer . . . *Wait,* he told himself.

The two officers were talking to one another in their own language that J. C. couldn't understand. The four escorts rode relaxed in their saddles, staring straight ahead with their rifles lying across their saddles, obviously not at all concerned about an ambush.

When they were only fifteen yards away, he feathered the trigger of his rifle. One of the guards was blown from his saddle. J. C. immediately dropped his long rifle and snatched up his pistol, aimed, and shot two more of the guards from his prone position.

Before the last shot found its mark, he leaped to his feet and rushed forward toward the surprised Mexicans. He motioned with the barrel of his pistol for them to raise their hands—they did.

He cautiously approached them. They sat nervously in their saddles with their hands raised. He paused with his pistol pointed point-blank at the frightened guard, knowing what the Captain had said, but unsure if he could actually do what he had been ordered to do.

For a long moment, he stared at the man. He was young, most likely not much older than J. C.

The Captain's orders were to take no prisoners unless they were officers. I have no choice except to kill this man.

He thumbed back the hammer of his pistol and aimed it at the young Mexican's forehead.

I can't do it! he thought. *I can't kill this young Mexican for no reason! He's done nothing to me to cause me to kill him. Somewhere, he's got family that loves him and worries about him, maybe even a wife and children.*

Reaching a hand, he jerked the man's rifle off the saddle in front of him and smashed it against a nearby rock. He motioned with his pistol for the man to dismount.

The young soldier quickly complied. J. C. lifted an arm and pointed in the direction from which they came. The young Mexican got the message and started backing away. When just a few steps had separated them, the Mexican turned and started running as fast as he could.

J. C. turned his attention to the two officers. He motioned for them to dismount. Holding his pistol on them, he removed their side arms. One of them had a Paterson revolver, much like J. C.'s own, except this one had a pearl handle. He shoved it down behind his belt.

The other officer carried a strange-looking pistol. He decided to keep it also. He searched their boots for any hide-out weapons but found nothing. He sliced two short pieces of leather from the young guard's saddle and tied the officers' hands securely behind their backs.

The sun was noon-high when he located Capt. Walker with his two captured Mexican officers in tow.

"Well, well, well! What you got here, Ranger?" Capt. Walker asked.

"Captured these officers headin' toward Texas; figured you'd want to have a talk with them."

Capt. Walker looked them up and down, smiling and nodding his head.

"You figured right. You got yourself some *big fish* here, Ranger Holderfield. *Big fish,* indeed. One's a colonel and the other's a major. Were they alone?"

"Uh, no, sir, they had four escorts riding with them."

"And you took care of all four single-handed? Well done, Ranger, well done. I think the general might want to have a talk with these fellows," he said, nodding agreement with himself. "Ranger Dean, accompany Ranger Holderfield as he transports the prisoners to Gen. Taylor's camp. Ranger Holderfield, deliver the prisoners *only* to the general himself, understand? Tell him all you have discovered."

"Yes, sir."

He took a moment to cinch the girth tighter on his saddle while Ranger Dean readied his own mount. They rode at a short lope with the two prisoners' horses on lead lines.

"Where's Gen. Taylor's headquarters?" he asked a guard at the edge of the vast camp.

The guard pointed down a long opening between two rows of tents.

"Down that'a way."

J. C. reined Blackie down the opening. Ranger Dean followed with the two prisoners in tow. Finally, he located a large tent with two flags in front. Two guards stood in front of the tent with rifle butts against the ground. He swung from the saddle.

"I'm Ranger Holderfield of the Texas Rangers. I have a report from Capt. Walker. I need to see Gen. Taylor."

"Wait right there," one of the guards said, eyeing the two prisoners before turning. He entered the tent and emerged almost immediately.

"He'll see you."

J. C. hurried through the flaps of the tent. Brigadier General Zachary Taylor sat behind a desk smoking a fat cigar.

J. C. saluted the way he remembered Capt. Walker saluting earlier. The general nodded and returned the salute.

"Ranger J. C. Holderfield reporting, sir. Capt. Walker sends his regards. We have sighted an army unit of thirty-four hundred men on foot, along with four heavy artillery pieces and two hundred cavalry moving towards the river. I also captured two Mexican officers. Capt. Walker said he figured you might want to talk to them."

"*You* captured two Mexican officers? Tell me about it, Ranger."

J. C. briefly related the incident, omitting the fact that he had released one of the escorts. As he talked, the General listened intently and nodded his approval.

"Well done, Ranger Holderfield, well done. I'd like to see these prisoners. Bring them in."

He stepped to the flap of the tent and motioned to Ranger Dean to bring the prisoners in. J. C. happened to be looking at the general's face when the prisoners walked in, escorted by Ranger Dean and one of the guards from the front of the tent. He saw General Taylor's eyes widen in surprise.

"Guard," the general said. "Go find my scout and bring him here."

In short minutes a rugged, whiskered old fellow in fringed, deerskin clothing stepped through the opening of the general's tent. He carried a Kentucky long rifle identical to the one J. C. carried. A long, wide-bladed knife rode in a leather scabbard on his wide belt.

"Mr. Doggett, these two prisoners possess valuable information that could possibly save hundreds, perhaps thousands, of American lives. I want to know everything they know about anything, understand?"

The old fellow slanted a hard look at the two captives, lifted the hint of a grin, and nodded. He shoved them ahead of him as they left the tent without a word.

J. C. could only imagine what the two Mexican officers were in for before the old scout secured the information the General wanted.

"Ranger Holderfield, you have performed an invaluable service to the cause. I won't forget it. See to your horse, Ranger, and then go eat and get some rest. We'll be moving out at first light. You'll ride with us."

"Yes, sir," he replied, again saluting.

After feeding, watering, and rubbing down their horses, J. C. and Ranger Dean ate their fill in the chow hall and even managed to stow away a half-dozen left-over biscuits. A friendly master sergeant showed them a tent they could bed down in. They found an empty cot and were asleep almost before their eyes closed.

A loud bugle blowing *reveille* woke them from a sound sleep. They immediately rose, stomped on their boots, dressed, and snatched up their rifles as they hurried from the tent.

All around them, soldiers were rushing to take down the tents, pack everything up, and prepare to move the entire army. They hurried to the corral and caught their horses. They were both saddled up and ready to ride by the time the soldiers formed up.

J. C. didn't know exactly where they were supposed to be in the large assembly. They sat their horses and waited. Soon, Gen. Taylor, accompanied by a dozen or more officers, rode past. One of the officers reined his mount around and rode up to J. C. and Ranger Dean. "The General wants both of you to ride with the officers at the head of the column."

J. C. swung a surprised look at Ranger Dean before heeling Blackie to follow the officer. As they caught up with the leaders of the long column, Gen. Taylor waved them over.

"Thanks to you, we've learned that the prisoners you captured were high ranking officers in General Mariano Arista's Army which is in route to lay siege upon Fort Texas, across the river from Matamoros. We're moving to reinforce the fort now.

"I've sent a dispatch to Capt. Walker requesting your service as part of my personal security force. Your bravery in capturing the two prisoners speaks well for the Texas Rangers and for your personal commitment to our cause.

"Both you and your companion will ride with me wherever I go and make yourselves available to whatever security needs I have. Is this agreeable?"

"Yes, sir, of course. We're here to serve."

"Well said, Ranger Holderfield, well said. Carry on."

**AUTHOR'S NOTE:*

The Mexican-American War lasted two years, from 1846-1848. Ranger Herb Dean requested a transfer back to the Texas Ranger Company after two months. His request was granted and he fought alongside Captain Samuel Walker until the captain was killed during the battle of *Huamantla, Mexico* on October 9th, 1847.

J. C. Holderfield remained with General Zachary Taylor for the duration of the war as part of the general's personal security force. He participated in the battles of *Palo Alto, Monterrey, Veracruz,* and *Buena Vista.*

During the *Battle of Buena Vista,* Mexican General *Antonio Lopez de Santa Anna,* with a force of 20,000 men, attacked Gen. Taylor's army and overran their position. Ranger Holderfield personally saved Gen. Taylor's life during the battle by killing six Mexican soldiers.

The war ended with the signing of the *Treaty of Guadalupe Hidalgo* on February 2, 1848, which established the *Rio Grande River* as the official border between the United States and Mexico.

As part of the treaty agreement, for the sum of $15,000,000, Mexico ceded the present states of California, Nevada, Utah, and parts of Colorado, Arizona, New Mexico, and Wyoming to the United States.

General Zachary Taylor was acclaimed by the press as a hero of the war and went on to become the twelfth President of the United States.

After the war, J. C. Holderfield returned to duty as a Texas Ranger, but with Capt. Walker gone, he wasn't happy and resigned after a year.

CHAPTER X

Following his resignation from the Texas Rangers, J. C. Holderfield had no idea what he would do or where he would go. He rode into the small town of San Antonio in June of 1849 searching for work. He was seventeen years old.

San Antonio had been ravaged by the war and reduced to a population of slightly over six hundred, most of whom were Mexican. He had little hope of finding work here, but he figured he had to start someplace.

The general mercantile store loomed larger than J. C. figured a town of this size should support. It was an *adobe* structure with a wide porch that stretched along the entire front of the building. Wooden barrels of ax, shovel, and hoe handles filled the barrels that sat along the porch. He reined up and tied Blackie to the hitching rail.

A tall, skinny fellow with a balding head and an apron tied around his middle greeted him.

"Howdy, stranger," the man said, looking over a pair of wire-rimmed spectacles. "How can I help you?"

"Looking for work."

"You and a whole passel of other folks. 'Fraid the pickin's are mighty slim in these parts. What kind of work you looking fer, young fellow?"

"Might near anything. I've been a Texas Ranger the last couple of years fighting with General Zachary Taylor."

"You don't say. You fought with *Old Rough and Ready* huh? Is he as tough as they say?"

"Tougher."

"So you're a lawman then?"

"I reckon you could say that."

"I hear Jessie Hoyt, over at the freight company, is looking for drivers. Wouldn't recommend it though; the last two got themselves killed on their first run."

"What's he hauling?"

"Don't seem to matter none. Mexicans kill the drivers and steal whatever they're hauling, wagon, team and all."

"Much obliged. I'll go talk to him."

"Be a crying shame to make it through the war and get yourself killed driving a freight wagon."

"Yeah, it would. Say I should talk to Jessie Hoyt?"

"Yep. Good luck to you young fellow, you'll be needin' it."

J. C. turned and left the store. He untied his horse and led it down the street to a small building that identified itself on a faded sign as the Hoyt Freighting Company. He tied his gelding to the hitching rail out front and went inside.

A paunchy fellow glanced up from behind a small desk as J. C. walked in.

"Can I help you?" the man asked.

"You Jessie Hoyt?"

"That's me. What can I do for you?"

"Looking for work. Fellow over at the store said you might be hiring drivers."

"Maybe. You ever drive a freight wagon?"

"Drove wagons all my life. Reckon one wagon drives pretty much like another. Been with the Texas Rangers for two years during the war until a week or so ago."

"Rangers, huh? Did the storekeeper tell you anything about the job?"

"He said your drivers keep getting themselves shot."

"That scare you?"

"I don't scare easy. What does the job pay?"

"Depends on the run. Round trip to Corpus Christi pays fifty dollars. Takes about ten days, more or less."

"What you hauling?"

"Bales of hides, mostly for shipment back east. On the return trip, we haul back supplies for the Army forts scattered around Texas."

"How often you have a run like that?"

"As often as you can handle."

"I'll take the job. When do I start?"

"Be here at first light in the morning."

"Count on it."

J. C. shook hands with his new employer and left. He headed for a livery stable and blacksmith shop that he had spotted earlier.

After securing a stall for Blackie and providing a generous portion of grain, J. C. headed for the small, box-like hotel up the street. He checked in, paid the dollar charge, and went to the room the fellow pointed to. He propped his Kentucky long rifle in the corner, laid his possibles bag beside the bed, and felt the cornshuck mattress with a hand.

How long has it been since I slept on a genuine mattress? he asked himself, but couldn't even remember the last time.

Fishing his money from his possibles bag, he stuffed it into his pocket and headed to the small café he had seen earlier.

He walked in and sat down at one of the three tables in the small room. A heavy-set, middle-aged woman with a dirty apron ambled up and wiped the dust from the table with a damp dish rag.

"What you got for supper?" he asked.

"Beef stew and sourdough biscuits, take it or leave it," she replied curtly.

"I'll take it."

The woman nodded and waddled off toward the kitchen. In short order she returned with a bowl of steaming stew and a straw basket full of biscuits. She set a jar of honey on the table and poured him a cup of coffee without bothering to ask.

"Much obliged," he said, picking up the spoon and stirring the stew to cool it.

"Ain't seen you around town before," she said.

He shook his head as he spooned a mouthful of stew. It tasted surprisingly good.

"Just rode in today."

"Looking fer work like everybody else in town?"

Again he shook his head.

"Nope. Got one. Driving freight for Jessie Hoyt."

"Then you better enjoy your last meal, stranger. His drivers have a way of getting shot."

"That's what I hear."

The woman walked away shaking her head. He finished his bowl of stew and ordered another. After cleaning the second bowl and, downing most of a pot of coffee, he pushed from the chair.

"How much?"

"Dollar," the woman replied.

"It was worth two," he told her.

He dropped two dollars on the table and walked from the café.

J. C. returned to his hotel room, locked the door, and laid all three of his pistols on the bed. He carefully loaded his two new ones, plus the one Capt. Walker had given him. He paused to look long at it.

How many men have I killed with this—too many to count. Funny, the only one he really remembered was the young Mexican soldier he didn't kill, the one he let go when he captured the Mexican officers—so long ago—all the rest were just faceless enemies.

Lying there in the darkness, his mind flashed back to Opal. He reached a hand and withdrew the yellow ribbon Opal had given him just before he left—the one he had carried all through the war.

As was his custom, he rose well before daylight, dressed, strapped on his guns, and went to make his first run as a freight driver. He stopped by the livery, saddled Blackie, filled his two canteens with fresh water from the livery well, and led his horse up the street to the freight office.

A heavily-loaded freight wagon like none he had ever seen stood waiting. Even a tall man like himself was dwarfed when standing beside the wheel. The wagon itself would easily hold what it would take four normal wagons to haul. The load of freight was covered with a large canvas, but J. C. could see bales of various kinds of hides showing under the edge of the covering. He saw buffalo, beaver, and deer hides.

There must be thousands of hides; a load that size would be worth a small fortune.

No wonder bandits are stealing his loads, he thought.

Three teams of heavy horses were hitched to the wagon and stood waiting. He tied his gelding on a lead line behind the wagon, opened the door of the freight office, and stepped inside. Jessie Hoyt was scribbling something on a freight bill by lamplight.

"Mornin'," the freight owner greeted. "Glad to see you didn't back out on the job."

"When I give my word, I keep it," J. C. told him, walking over to a pot-belly stove and pouring himself a cup of coffee from a blackened pot. He took a sip of the strong coffee and shook his head.

"That'll wake a fellow up."

"Outta be fresh," Hoyt said. "Made it just yesterday, I think it was. This freight bill shows what's on your load. Have Sam Hicks at the Steamship Lines in Corpus Christi sign it and bring it back to me. He'll have a return load for the military waiting for you, too.

"Good luck, Mr. Holderfield. Hope you don't run into trouble."

"Yeah, me too. Much obliged for the job, Mr. Hoyt. I'll do my best."

"Somehow, I believe that. I think you're that kind of man."

They shook hands. J. C. left the office, lifted his Kentucky long rifle into the wagon and climbed up into the seat. He propped his rifle beside him, gathered the three sets of long reins, let off the brake, and popped the reins.

"Hee-yaw! Get up in there!" he hollered.

The teams lunged into their collars. Trace chains went taut, and the heavy wagon moved forward—the long, hundred-forty mile journey to Corpus Christi had begun.

Many, many wagons had gone before him, packing the sandy soil rock hard, yet the large, iron-clad wheels of the heavy freight wagon cut deep scars in the heavily-traveled road leading out of San Antonio.

The six freight horses set their own pace, familiar with both the weight of the load and the route. They made it look almost effortless as they plodded steadily along.

J. C. quickly settled into the rhythm of the movement, but kept a sharp eye on the road ahead. The country was mostly flat and sandy with sparse vegetation. There were a few scrawny mesquite trees growing in scattered clusters. Here and there a rocky finger poked through the side of a small hillside. Dry arroyos snaked across the barren landscape bearing witness of ancient waterways, long since only a forgotten memory.

Sunrise brought with it a blazing sun. Shimmering heat waves lifted in the distance. Even the slight breeze brought with it temperatures that baked everything it touched.

By noon, he hit the Atascosa River just as Hoyt said he would. According to the freight owner, he would follow the river all the way to Corpus Christi.

J. C. sleeved sweat from his forehead with the swipe of an arm. The image of Opal Sullivan flashed from his memory.

Wonder how she's doing? How long has it been? Three years? Has it been that long since I told her goodbye and rode away with a promise to return? Wonder if she's still waiting for me?—most likely not. She's probably already married and has a family by now.

Nonetheless, the memory of her was one of the few good things in his life.

Now and then he glanced quickly up at the sun to measure its path across the sky. Noonday turned to late afternoon. He stopped at a sloping bank of the river to allow the horses to slake their thirst before moving on. The large wheels of the wagon left miles in their path as the sun approached the western horizon. Up ahead, he saw a cluster of large boulders near the edge of the water that offered a measure of protection for both him and his horses. He reined through an opening between two giant boulders and pulled the teams to a stop.

After unhitching the horses and watering them and his own mount, he tied them securely to the wagon wheels and built a small fire. He took supplies from his pack and made coffee.

As darkness deepened, he fried potatoes and salt pork and sipped coffee as supper cooked. He scooped a helping into his tin plate and began eating. The sound of approaching horses interrupted his meal.

Setting down his plate and coffee cup, he snatched up his loaded Kentucky long rifle, as well as the extra one he had brought along. He ducked behind a chest-high rock, set the extra rifle within easy reach, and waited. His three Paterson Colt pistols were also loaded and ready.

They rode in at full gallop, but reined up hard and fanned out when they approached his campfire. By light of a full moon, J. C. counted seven of them; all appeared to be Mexican, all hard-looking men who seemed the kind that would sell their own mother for a few *pesos.*

The obvious leader rode a snow-white gelding with a showy, silver Concho-studded saddle. He was a small man, dressed in black pants, white silk shirt with ruffles down the front, and embroidered waist jacket. He wore two, ivory-handled Paterson revolvers.

His companions all wore typical peasant clothes. To a man, they carried an assortment of rifles of one kind or another. Their heads swiveled to and fro, searching for the driver who dared bring a load of furs into their territory.

"Hey, *Amigo!* Why you hide?" the leader asked. "Come out and be friendly. All we want is a cup of your coffee, *si?"*

J. C. raised his head and shoulders above the top of the boulder. He laid his rifle on top of the rock with his finger on the trigger and the nose centered on the leader's chest.

The move drew every gaze to fix squarely on him.

"Ain't feeling especially friendly tonight," J. C. replied. "You boys best move on before somebody gets hurt."

An overdone smile revealed two gold teeth side by side in the very front of the leader's mouth. His smile belied the cold, icy stare from coal-black eyes—as cold as a tombstone.

"Aaah, *gringo,* I see you bring *Angel Aguilar* another load of furs! *Gracias tanto!* You leave now, I let you live. You stay, you die!"

"Tell you what, *amigo!* Since we're making *deals,* I'll make you one. My rifle's aimed squarely at your chest. You and your men drop your weapons and climb down off your horses, and you can all walk away. If you don't, you'll be the first one to die, *comprenda?"*

J. C.'s words clearly surprised the arrogant leader. His eyes widened, his head jerked quick looks at his companions as if to say *this isn't the way this was supposed to work.*

For a long moment, all seven bandits sat nervously, waiting for their leader to tell them what to do. Then, the leader spread his open hands in a gesture of giving up, licked his dry lips, and with a shaky voice, said, "You win this round, *gringo,* but we'll be back!"

"NO! That wasn't my offer. If you so much as breathe deep, I'll blow you clean out of that fancy saddle! NOW DO LIKE I SAID OR DIE! That's my final offer." Even in the light from the moon, J. C. could see the big beads of sweat that popped out on the bandit's forehead. He could also see the sheer hatred in his eyes.

J. C. tightened his finger on the trigger of his rifle, feeling sure the leader would try something. A long, nervous moment passed. Finally, the bandit barked an order in *Spanish.*

"Haga Como dice, déjà caer sus armas y se baja!" The other bandits looked confused. They exchanged questioning glances with their comrades and delayed too long to satisfy the clearly worried leader.

"IAHORA!"

One by one the bandits reluctantly dropped their rifles and climbed to the ground. The leader still sat motionless.

"You, too!" J. C. said calmly.

Slowly, cautiously, the leader stepped from his horse to the ground.

"Unbuckle them pistols, let 'em drop, and start walking. If I see hide or hair, I'll kill you on sight!"

The embarrassed leader did as he was told. He had been humiliated in front of his men and would have to retaliate somehow—but how? J. C. knew he hadn't seen the last of *Angel Aguilar.*

J. C. remained where he was and watched as the seven bandits slowly turned and walked away, leaving their horses and weapons. His slow gaze swept the surrounding darkness for an hour, half expecting one or more of the bandits to make a try for their weapons—or him, but he saw no movement. He was under no illusions that they had given up so easily—they'd be back.

He didn't allow himself to sleep a wink that night. All night he hunkered down, waiting for them to attack, but the sanctuary of daylight finally arrived; at least now he could see any danger approaching. Only after full daylight did he venture from his hiding place, and then with great caution.

He gathered the weapons they left and piled them under the wagon seat. He loosened the cinch straps and left the bandits' saddles lying on the ground, except for the fancy one that had belonged to the leader—he loaded that one onto the wagon. It would bring a good price and an extra bonus for the aggravation *Angel Aguilar* and his men had caused.

He tied the seven horses behind the wagon with Blackie and hitched the teams to the wagon.

He pulled away from the campsite, watching nervously, but still saw no sign of the bandits. Only after he had put several miles behind him did he begin to relax.

As the day wore on and the heat increased, his eyes got heavy. He knew he couldn't afford to doze off. He splashed water from his canteen on his face to keep himself awake. Miles were left in his back trail. Somehow he managed to stay awake. Finally, the afternoon sun dipped behind the horizon.

The country had changed drastically during the day. Left behind was the sandy country. It was replaced by flat prairie with lush, green grass. Giant oak trees spread their limbs in a wide circle—truly it was prime cattle country—the kind of country where a man could put down roots and raise a family.

That thought brought Opal back to his mind. It seemed he was thinking more and more about her lately.

A small grove of maple saplings beside the river seemed like a good place to stop for the night. He reined the heavy wagon to a stop. He paused to survey the surrounding area. He could see for miles in any direction. He was satisfied no one could approach without his knowledge. He watered all his stock and tied them on a long rope line stretched between two trees with enough slack to allow them to graze.

Only after all the chores were finished did he make camp, put on coffee, and cook supper. The hot coffee bought him some time, but long before the campfire had burned down, he was sound asleep with his rifles within reach.

The night passed without incident. As was his custom, he woke before daylight, walked down to the river, removed his shirt, and washed himself in the chilly water.

After breakfast and several cups of coffee, he felt almost normal again. He took his time watering the horses and hitching the teams to the wagon. The sun was an hour old when he climbed into the wagon and again headed southeast along the river.

On the fourth day after leaving San Antonio, he pulled his teams to a stop outside the Steamship Lines in Corpus Christi. A fellow a head taller than himself walked out to meet him.

"You from Jessie Hoyt's freight line in San Antonio?" the big man asked.

"Yep. Got a load of furs," J. C. told him, handing the man the freight bill Mr. Hoyt had given him.

"Where'd you get the horses?" the man asked, taking the freight bill and glancing at the horses tied behind the wagon.

"Picked 'em up along the way," J. C. said, not elaborating on the subject.

"Uh, huh," the man said, lifting a knowing grin.

"Mighty fancy saddle there on the back of the wagon, too. Don't see many like that in these parts."

"I thought so, too. Got any idea where I might sell some of the horses and the saddle?"

"Might try the livery—two streets over and north a few blocks. Talk to Lester Phillips. He'll treat you fair."

"Much obliged."

"We'll unload your wagon and reload it with the supplies for the army while you're going over to Phillips' place. It'll be loaded and ready to roll by the time you get back."

J. C. saddled Blackie and put the fancy saddle on the outlaw leader's horse. He strung them all on a lead line and headed toward the livery.

Lester Phillips was a short, bald headed fellow with an honest-looking face. He walked from the double doors of the livery and stopped in front of the string of horses.

"Howdy," the liveryman greeted.

"Howdy," J. C. said, returned the greeting. "Fellow over at the Steamship Lines said you might be interested in buying some horses," J. C. told him.

"Might. What you askin'?"

"What you payin'?" J. C. countered.

The liveryman walked slowly around the seven horses, examining them closely. He spat a stream of brown tobacco juice and looked J. C. square in the eye.

"Tell you like it is, young fellow. Don't know where you got them and don't care, but these animals have been abused something awful. I can count the ribs on might near every one of 'em. I couldn't offer more'n twenty dollars apiece fer them. I'll go thirty on the white gelding."

"I'll take it. What about the saddle?"

"Now that's something else again. Ain't seen one like that in a coon's age. I'll give you fifty dollars fer it."

"Sold," J. C. told him.

"Come on inside and I'll get your money."

Five minutes later, he left the livery with two hundred dollars in his pocket. He rode back to the Steamship Lines feeling good and arrived as two workers were tying down the canvas over the return load.

"What's in the load?" he asked the Steamship foreman.

"It's a shipment of brand new guns and ammunition going to the army from Colt Arms Company in Hartford, Connecticut. I'd be mighty careful on the trip home if I was you. Lots of folks would like to get their hands on this shipment."

"Looks to me like the army would provide an armed escort if this load is so valuable."

"Seems like it, don't it?"

He thanked the foreman, tied Blackie behind the wagon, and climbed up into the driver's seat. He popped the reins and the big horses responded—he was headed home—home—but where was his *home?*

CHAPTER XI

The return load was even heavier than the load of furs. The wagon wheels cut deep ruts in the road. J. C. thought about the load he carried. What the foreman said was true. Road bandits would go to any lengths to get their hands on a load of guns and ammunition if they knew what he carried.

He was extra cautious as he traveled. His head swiveled back and forth, constantly on the alert for any sign of danger.

Just a few miles outside Corpus Christi he encountered the thickets. The almost impenetrable mesquite and underbrush were so dense no horse and rider could penetrate them.

They hugged the narrow road on both sides and were the home of millions of longhorn cattle that had lived in the thickets so long they were as vicious and dangerous as any wild animal. He relaxed somewhat, knowing it would be next to impossible for anyone to hide in the thickets waiting to ambush him.

It was full dark by the time he cleared the thickets. Once again, he followed the open road that ran alongside the Atascosa River. He searched the darkness for a suitable place to stop for the night that offered some measure of protection.

It was late when he finally located a small clearing in a heavy growth of giant oak trees a small distance from the river's edge. He decided that would have to do and pulled the heavy freight wagon into the clearing.

After unhitching the teams, he led them, along with Blackie, to the river to water. He tied them to the wagon wheels and built a small fire close to the wagon. He put on water for coffee and settled down with his back against one of the wagon wheels. He was tired and hungry. He had cured ham and fried potatoes for supper and washed it down with several cups of coffee. Afterward, he settled down on his bedroll with his rifle to get some sleep.

Distant thunder woke him sometime during the night. The smell of rain was strong on the southern wind that whipped about him. He quickly gathered his bedroll and moved it underneath the wagon.

Lightning stabbed the earth like jagged lances from dark clouds and lit the night as if it were day. Deafening thunder rolled like echoes of cannon fire and shook the ground. The heavens opened and a heavy rain hit like water poured from a bucket. The remainder of the night was wet and miserable.

It was still raining hard when daylight came. He decided to wait awhile and see if it let up before continuing his journey. He huddled underneath the wagon and watched it rain. The water quickly filled the low-lying swags and would certainly slow progress for his trip home.

He estimated it to be near noonday before the rain slackened. He crawled out from under the wagon, rolled his bedroll, and hitched the teams to the wagon.

The rain had softened the ground and the wheels of the heavy wagon buried deep. The teams struggled to keep the wagon moving. He stopped frequently to allow the teams to rest before moving on.

Nightfall came and he estimated he had made no more than a dozen miles. He camped that night in a growth of sycamore trees only fifty yards from the river. The night passed without incident and before daylight the next morning he was on the road.

The sun of the afternoon before had dried out the road and he was making good progress.

He was coming into the area where the road bandits had attacked him on the trip down; he hoped they had learned their lesson. Nonetheless, he nervously watched both sides of the road, alert for trouble.

It came unexpectedly. Rifle shots blasted from the left side of the road and buried in the wooden side of the wagon. The bandits boiled from a cluster of rocks that lined both sides of the road.

J. C. popped the reins and hollered at the three teams of horses. A barrage of rifle and pistol shots blasted from the outlaws. Slugs tore into the loaded wagon and buzzed past his head. He slid down to the floor between the seat and the front of the wagon, snatched up his long rifle with one hand, and sent a rifle ball at the charging bandits behind him.

Quickly glancing around for a place of safety, he spotted a cluster of house-size boulders scattered along the top of a hillside half-a-hundred yards to his right—he reined the teams in that direction.

The three teams struggled mightily to pull the heavily-loaded wagon up the hillside, but finally made it. He guided them into a small open clearing among the rocks. Snatching up his rifle, he leaped from the wagon and took shelter behind a large rock.

Glancing up, he saw eight mounted riders charging up the hillside toward him. He hurriedly loaded his long rifle, took aim, and blew one of the riders from his saddle. The bandit bounced and tumbled along the ground. His riderless horse veered off to the right, its reins dragging the ground.

The bandits were getting too close for him to reload his rifle. He flung it aside and snatched two of his Paterson Colt pistols from their holsters and began firing with both guns.

He didn't have time to watch the results of his shots, but with each pull of the trigger, he swung his pistols to find two new targets. Suddenly, the remaining riders swerved their mounts and headed back down the hill. He counted only four riders still in their saddles.

He watched them as they assembled on the road below. A fifth man emerged from the rocks carrying a rifle.

Still outnumbered five to one, he considered. *Not good odds—not good odds at all.*

He reloaded all of his weapons and prepared for what he knew would come. He watched the bandits below; it was the same bunch he had encountered earlier.

They split up and circled wide out of range before climbing the hill on foot. It was clear they intended to get behind him. He watched carefully, trying as best he could to keep track of each man's location, but he soon lost sight of them—all he could do was watch and wait.

All was quiet for a half-hour. He leaned his back against a large boulder and swept the boulders above him for any sign of the bandits.

He heard the shot at the same instant he felt the singe of the rifle ball that sped past and ricocheted off the rock only inches from his head. Instinctively, he ducked and snapped off shots from both his Paterson pistols at a spot just below the rising puff of smoke. As he fired, he threw his body into a roll and came to rest several feet away beside another boulder. More shots blasted and lead balls gouged chips from the boulder he had just vacated.

For the next hour, they exchanged shots as fast as he changed locations. Three times he reloaded all three pistols. When he reached for ammunition again, he discovered to his horror that his possibles bag was empty. A surge of fear swept through him.

Darkness was fast approaching. He knew without a doubt they would come for him with the darkness.

If I'm out of ammunition, I'm a dead man!

That's when it dawned on him that he had a whole wagon load of both guns and ammunition!

Maybe I can slip one of the crates off the wagon in the darkness and locate some more ammunition before they move in for the kill.

He eyed the wagon that sat no more than twenty feet away—but that twenty feet was across open ground with no cover.

He checked his guns. He had enough powder for one more load of his rifle. Two of his pistols were empty. The third one had only two loads left—three more shots—only three more shots left!

Can I make it to the wagon and get more ammunition before they come?—I've got no choice—I've got to!

He carefully examined the open space between him and the wagon in relation to the location of the bandits as indicated by their shots. They had open shots for the entire twenty feet—it would be like shooting fish in a water trough—still, he had to try.

He pulled his feet underneath him, took a deep breath, and shot to his feet.

Immediately a shot blasted! The familiar whine of the slug ricocheted off the rock behind him. A volley of shots dug furrows in the dirt all around him. He kept his head down and ran with all his might.

While still several yards from the wagon, he dove headlong toward the space between the large wheels—and safety. He landed flat on his stomach. The impact knocked the wind out of him—but he was safe—at least for now.

For a moment he lay motionless, using the time to get his breath back. He belly-crawled to the back of the wagon. Rising cautiously, he chanced a quick look—the wagon was between him and the bandits.

He used his knife to cut the rope that secured the canvas and raised the corner. A large, wooden crate was stacked on top of three other similar ones. The stenciled black letters on top of the crate identified the contents as .44 caliber revolver ammunition.

.44 caliber? His pistols were all .36 caliber—the ammunition wouldn't work in his weapons!

He quickly pulled down the other three crates underneath the first—they were all the same. The crates behind the ammunition boxes were a different size. He decided to check those, too. He pulled the top crate off—it was even heavier than the others.

The stencil on top identified the contents as .44 caliber Colt Dragoon Revolvers.

He pried the top from the crate. Dozens and dozens of small, polished wood boxes were stacked neatly in the large crate. He quickly opened one of the boxes. The box contained a large, long-barrel revolver with a walnut handle. He snatched it up—it was heavy—he judged it to be near four pounds. He noticed right away that the revolving cylinder held six shots instead of his Paterson's five.

The heavy Colt Dragoons were awkward and cumbersome at first, the heavier weight and length of the barrel, which he judged to be over seven inches, made handling it more difficult, but he could quickly see that the extra firepower was a real advantage. He would just have to get used to the differences and practice even harder.

What a beautiful weapon! he thought.

He quickly tore two more boxes open, laying the three revolvers on the tailgate of the wagon. Then he pried open one of the ammunition crates and quickly loaded all three of the new revolvers.

It was full dark by the time he finished. A three-quarter moon offered little light in a cloudy sky. With his three, fully-loaded revolvers, he ducked back underneath the wagon—and none too soon.

The soft crunch of a boot on loose pebbles reached his hearing—they were coming!

He waited . . .

Again he heard the sound of footsteps—this time even closer.

He drew back the hammers of two of his new revolvers, took a deep breath, and waited.

The shadowy outline of two men crept slowly toward the wagon. Each one carried a rifle in his hands. J. C. peered through the spokes of a big wheel, gripping the pistols in his hands until his hands grew sweaty.

When they were only steps from the wagon, he fired both revolvers at the same time. The twin blasts were deafening. Both bandits were lifted off their feet by the force of the heavy .44 slugs. They sprawled in the dirt and didn't move.

Two down and three to go, he thought.

"Paco, es usted bien?" a voice from the darkness called.

It sounded like the same voice he remembered from his earlier encounter. After a moment, he heard what sounded like the same, muffled, angry voice giving an order.

The vague silhouette of three men appeared in the distance—one carried a rifle, one a machete, and the last a handgun. They were headed for his wagon.

Again he raked back the hammers of both guns with his thumbs, waited and watched.

Angel Aguilar hung back, letting his two men lead the way. They moved cautiously, their heads swiveling to and fro, unsure where their enemy was hiding.

"¡Bajo el vagon! ¡Matelo!" the leader suddenly shouted, lifting his pistol.

The words were barely out of the outlaw's mouth when J. C. fired both of the Colt Dragoons at the same time. They were the last words *Angel Aguilar* would ever speak. The only bandit left standing was the one with the machete in his hand.

J. C. crawled out from under the wagon, keeping both guns pointed squarely at the outlaw. The frightened man dropped the machete and stood motionless, waiting for his fate.

J. C. rose to his feet and walked slowly toward the man. He slanted a look at *Aguilar* squirming in pain on the ground from a gut-shot. He kicked the pistol out of the bandit's reach and stared down at him.

"I told you if I ever seen you again I'd kill you," J. C. told him. "You should'a listened."

"Por favor, Senor, no me mata," the only remaining bandit begged.

"Go," J. C. said, motioning with his pistol.

"¡Gracias, Senor, gracias! Mi esposa y los ninos, gracias!"

J. C. had learned enough Mexican during the war to understand that the man's wife and children thanked him for sparing his life.

After the surviving Mexican left on his horse, J. C. gathered the rest of the outlaw horses and weapons and tied the horses to the back of the wagon. He dragged the dead bandits together and laid them beside the dying leader. Then he packed away his Paterson pistols and replaced them with the Colt Dragoons.

Angel Aguilar alternated between begging for help, praying, and cursing the *Americano.*

By the time J. C. finished his supper and third cup of coffee, the bandit leader was dead.

It was quite a sight and one few San Antonio townspeople would soon forget.

The heavily-loaded freight wagon rolled slowly down the street. Behind it, eight horses were tied on lead lines. Eight Mexican bodies were tied belly down across their saddles.

J. C. pulled the wagon to a stop in front of the freight office. Jessie Hoyt stepped from the office to meet him. A large crowd of gawkers was gathering in and along the street.

"Whatcha got there, J. C.?" the freighter asked, looking over the dead men.

"Road bandits," he replied, climbing down from the wagon.

"Likely the same ones that's been hitting my wagons and killing my drivers?"

"Likely," J. C. said, using his coonskin cap to beat the dust from his clothes.

"How'd you manage to take them down all by yourself? That's amazing!"

"I just did what I had to do, that's all."

Jessie Hoyt nodded his head.

"Well, you shore did that, alright. When will you be ready for another run?"

"Give me a few hours shuteye and I'll be ready."

"I'll have a load ready for you at first light."

"I'll be here. Where can we dump these fellows? They're getting a little ripe."

"Go on and get some rest; I'll see they're taken care of."

"I'll be wanting to sell their horses," J. C. said.

"They'll be at the livery."

J. C. left the eight dead outlaws with the freight owner and rode Blackie to the livery stable. He stalled and fed his mount before heading for the hotel and securing a room.

The story of him killing the eight highway bandits all by himself spread through San Antonio like wildfire. Within hours, J. C. Holderfield was the talk of the town and San Antonio's most famous citizen.

J. C. made two more runs to Corpus Christi that month without any trouble. When he arrived back in San Antonio after his last haul, Jessie Hoyt told him there was a well-dressed fellow named Samuel Pryor in town wanting to talk with him.

"What's he want?" J. C. asked.

"Didn't figure it was any of my business so I didn't ask. He's staying over at the hotel."

"I'll look him up."

J. C. took Blackie to the livery and saw he was provided for before he went to the hotel.

"Understand there's a fellow named Pryor staying here?" he asked the clerk.

"Yes, sir, Mr. Holderfield, he's been here almost a week."

"Where is he now?"

"He left just a little while ago. He said he was going up to the café for supper."

J. C. walked up the street to the San Antonio Café and stepped inside. Only two tables were occupied. At one table sat an older couple. A fellow in a business suit sat at the other.

"Are you Sam Pryor?" J. C. asked as he stopped beside the man's table.

The man looked up from his supper and stood to his feet with his hand extended.

"Yes—yes, I am. And you must be Mr. Holderfield?"

J. C. took the man's hand in a firm handshake.

"Heard you were looking for me?"

"Yes—yes, would you join me? I was just having a bite of supper."

"Don't mind if I do."

He pulled out a chair and sat down. The heavy-set waitress hurried up.

"What'll you have?" she asked.

"Whatever he's having."

After the waitress left, J. C. looked Mr. Pryor over. He was an average sized, distinguished-looking fellow, well dressed, with salt and pepper hair. He wore a mustache on his top lip.

"What can I do for you, Mr. Pryor?" he asked.

"I'm here representing the town council of a community in east Texas called Dallas. Our community is new, founded only seven years ago at the ford of the Trinity River, but we are growing rapidly. Therein lies the problem.

"Our rapid growth has attracted an element of lawbreakers and ruffians that has gotten out of hand and is stifling our continued growth. Our citizens can't walk the streets without being verbally harassed and sometimes physically assaulted. We aren't even safe in our own homes at night. We are businessmen and family men. We can't stand up to these men. In short, we need help.

"Word reached us about your reputation in dealing with this type of men. We also understand you are a former Texas Ranger. We'd like to hire you as town marshal to come and clean up our community."

"I've already got a job," J. C. told him over the rim of his coffee cup.

"I understand. We're still a poor community, but I've been authorized to offer you *one hundred dollars* a month. We need you, Mr. Holderfield. Will you help us?"

J. C. stared at the coffee in his cup for a long minute without replying to the man's question.

I like my job driving freight, and counting the extra I've been making from selling outlaw horses, I'm making a good living, but I don't hanker driving a freight wagon the rest of my life.

They've made a good offer. Hard to turn down a hundred dollars a month. Besides, my heart is in law work and this seems like a good opportunity.

He looked up and fixed a stare into Mr. Pryor's eyes.

"I'll come on one condition. That I do things my way and that the town council or whatever group is doing the hiring backs me up. The day I don't get it, I'm gone. Agreed?"

"Agreed," Sam Pryor said, sticking out his hand for a handshake to seal the bargain. "When can you start?"

"I'll tell Mr. Hoyt I'm leaving. We can leave day after tomorrow, if that's agreeable?"

"Splendid. I'll be ready when you are."

CHAPTER XII

The community of Dallas had been laid out well. Streets were staked off, waiting for businesses to build on the empty lots. The main street connected with the ford across the Trinity River and it was clear that large numbers of wagons used the only crossing within a hundred miles.

The main street widened when it intersected the first cross street. An iron water pump and round, rock watering trough sat in the center of the intersection.

"That large building in the center of the block is John Bryan's mercantile store and trading post," Pryor explained as they rode into town. "John originally built it to trade with the *Caddo* Indians that lived in this area, but after the government moved them all out of Texas, he decided to build a permanent community here.

"John's our leading citizen. He's postmaster, store owner, head of our town council, ferry boat operator, and right now, he's the judge. That big house on the hill belongs to him."

"Sounds like a busy fellow," J. C. commented.

"That's Doctor Bixby's home and office over there," Pryor said, pointing to a well-kept, white frame house. "Fellow named Cantrell moved in a couple years ago. He's a lawyer. That's his office next door to the doctor. Booster Yates is our blacksmith and livery operator, and Miss Bell runs the Dinner Bell Cafe there. Reverend Brown came to town about a year ago and we built the church. Jeb Sawyer is on the council; he operates a sawmill down the river a couple of miles."

"Who runs the saloon?" J. C. asked, twisting a look at the large building across the street from the general store.

"That'd be Ike Booth. He's a big part of our problems. His place draws no-goods like a cow patty draws flies. They come from a hundred miles around and way too many of them decide to stay.

"Ike owns all them shanties the other end of town yonder, too. Folks hereabouts call it *Shanty Town*. He's got another saloon there. You can buy most anything in Shanty Town: women, opium, hire somebody killed—you name it, and it's for sale. There's so many shootings, they've even got their own *boot hill*. No decent person would even think of venturing down there."

As they rode past the saloon, J. C. saw two hard-case-looking fellows leaning against the front of the building. Both men gave him narrow-lidded stares—both wore tied-down Paterson pistols on their hips.

The two men hurried inside the saloon as J. C. and Pryor reined up across the street in front of Bryan's General Store.

"Come on," Pryor said. "I want you to meet John."

As they entered the crowded store, with supplies stacked from floor to ceiling, J. C. looked the storekeeper over. He was a slope-shouldered, well-fed forty-something who stood a hand over six feet and would weigh well over two hundred pounds. He had shoulder-length red hair, a full beard, and a no-nonsense look about him.

"John, this here is J. C. Holderfield, J. C., this is John Bryan."

They shared a firm handshake with steady gazes fixed on one another.

"Mighty pleased to meet you, Mr. Holderfield," the storekeeper said in a deep, gravely voice. "We're glad you're here."

"Howdy, Mr. Bryan."

"I'm sure Sam has filled you in about what you'll be facing. We need a man like you to clean things up around here and get rid of the riff-raff so decent folks ain't afraid to walk down the street."

"I'll do my best," J. C. told him.

"Here," Bryan said, handing J. C. a shiny new badge. "You are now our new town marshal."

"Do we have a jail?" J. C. asked.

Bryan and Pryor both exchanged surprised glances.

"Uh—well—no—we just haven't had a need for one yet," Bryan said.

"Build one," J. C. told them. "We're gonna need it."

"We'll have a town council meeting tonight. If you can, we'd like you to be there. I'd like to introduce you to everyone," Bryan said. "What else can we do to help?"

"Pass an ordinance making it against the law to carry a gun within town limits and have two signs made saying that. Put one on each end of town."

"We can pass the law; can you enforce it?"

"If I can't, you don't need me."

"I like your attitude, young fellow. Mind me asking how old you are?"

"I'm seventeen; does that make a difference?"

"You've built quite a reputation for seventeen. We don't give a whit how old you are as long as you can do the job."

"I'll do my best, Mr. Bryan. When and where is the meeting?"

"Good dark at my house."

"I'll be there," J. C. told him, reaching a hand. "Pleasure meeting you, Mr. Bryan."

"Call me John, everybody does."

"John it is then."

"I see you got a hotel, I'll be staying there until I can make other arrangements," J. C. said, touching the edge of his coonskin cap.

He untied Blackie and walked him down the street to the livery. A grizzly old fellow in bib overalls and work shirt was pitching hay into the corral where a half-dozen horses eagerly welcomed the food.

"Howdy," J. C. greeted.

The old liveryman leaned on his pitchfork and eyed J. C.

"You that new town marshal we been hearing about?"

"Reckon that's me. Name's Holderfield—J. C. Holderfield. You'd be Booster Yates."

"You're a mite young to be a lawman, ain't ye?"

"Don't reckon I knew age had anything to do with it. I was a Texas Ranger for almost three years and fought in the Mexican-American War with General Zachary Taylor."

"Young fellow, if you served with ole *Rough and Ready* that's all I need to know. Welcome to Dallas."

The liveryman stuck out a calloused hand. J. C. took it and shared a firm handshake.

"I'll be needing to stall my horse, with grain once a day. What will I owe you?"

"Fifty cents a day for stalling, grain once a day, and all the hay he can eat."

"Sounds fair. I'll be over at the hotel if you need me."

"Put your gelding right over there in that first stall. I'll take care of him from there."

J. C. led Blackie over to the stall, unsaddled him, brushed him down, and paid the liveryman fifteen dollars for the first month.

"Think I'll mosey up the street to that little café and stretch my britches."

"Miss Bell can shore do that, sure enough," the liveryman cackled.

J. C. sauntered casually up the street to the *Dinner Bell Café,* according to the sign over the door. He pushed it open and stepped inside.

The young lady who twisted a look at him was the prettiest lady he had ever seen! She was slim and shapely with long, blonde hair that hung in curls below her shoulders. It was gathered in the back and tied with a bright, green ribbon. Her jade-green eyes matched the ribbon and seemed to sparkle as she sent a smile toward him. Her pretty eyes lingered when she saw the badge pinned to his deerskin jacket.

"You couldn't be the lawman we've been hearing about," she said with a friendly voice.

"Why not?"

"Because you're—you're too young."

"How old do I need to be?"

"I—well, I don't know. It just surprised me that you're so young, that's all."

"Are you the Miss Bell they've been telling me about?"

"I am; May Bell Preston."

"I'm J. C. Holderfield. Pleased to meet you. You're younger than I thought you'd be, too."

"Why is that?"

"Well, with you owning your own business and all, I just figured you'd be older."

They both laughed at the situation.

"Okay, you win: so we're both old enough to do our job," she said, laughing. "Have a seat. I assume you came to have supper?"

"I sure did, ma'am. What would you recommend?"

"For a big lawman like you, I'd say you'd like a steak and all the trimmings. How would you like it cooked?"

"Ma'am, as long as it don't bellow when I stick a fork in it, I'll eat it."

"You got it. I'll get you some coffee."

She hurried into a smaller back room and emerged with a steaming coffee pot and a heavy, white mug. She poured it full and lingered for a long moment. A serious look suggested she wanted to say something that was stuck in her throat.

"Have they told you about all the trouble we've been having?"

"Yes, ma'am, that's why they hired me."

"You seem like a nice young man. Please be careful."

"I'm a careful kind of fellow," he assured her. She nodded and hurried to the kitchen to prepare his supper.

While he was sipping his hot coffee, the two mean-looking hombres he had seen earlier in front of the saloon walked in, eyed him, and sat down at one of the tables.

"Let's have some service out here!" one of them hollered loudly.

"I'll be right with you," the pretty lady said from the kitchen.

In a moment, she hurried out with two cups and a pot of coffee. She nodded to the men and lifted a small smile as she poured their coffee.

The younger of the two reached an arm and pulled her closer, letting his hand linger on her backside. She jerked away abruptly.

"Don't do that!" she said curtly.

"What's a matter? I ain't good enough for you?" he demanded, reaching out and capturing her wrist and jerking her up against him.

J. C. had seen enough. He pushed up from his chair, calmly walked over to the table, and looked down at the two men.

"The lady asked you to stop," he said through clenched teeth.

Both men shot looks up at him. The younger shoved Miss Bell away from him.

"Who are you?" the younger hombre demanded.

"This ain't none of your business!"

"I'm J. C. Holderfield, the new town marshal, and I'm making it my business."

Both men shoved up from their chairs at the same instant. J. C. saw their hands drop to the guns strapped to their sides. Before they could draw their pistols, his hand dipped, drew his Colt Dragoon, and swung it sideways. The blow from the heavy gun caught the younger fellow alongside the head and knocked him flat of his back.

With a continued motion, he swung the nose of his Colt to cover the other fellow. The man had his Paterson halfway out, but let it drop back into its holster as he stared down the barrel of the big .44 Colt Dragoon.

"Get your partner up off the floor," J. C. ordered.

"You're both under arrest."

"Under arrest?" the older fellow protested. "What for?"

"For molesting this young lady, that's what for. Now do like I said before I rap you on the head, too."

J. C. relieved both men of their side arms as the older fellow helped the younger one up off the floor.

"I'm sorry they bothered you, Miss Bell. Keep my steak warm. I'll be right back."

He marched the two men outside and down the street to Bryan's store.

"What's going on," Bryan asked when he marched the two men inside.

"I need two lengths of chain ten foot long and four locks."

The storekeeper looked confused, but hurried to get what J. C. asked for. He returned shortly and handed the items to the new lawman. Without further explanation, J. C. marched the two men outside and up the street to the rock fountain. John Bryan and several others followed to see what was going to happen. Several poured out of the saloon across the street to watch.

He looped one end of the chain around each man's ankle and locked it in place. The other end he wrapped around the iron pump and locked them.

"If you fellows tear the pump up, I'll keep you locked here another ten days."

"You can't do this!" they screamed. "This ain't human to chain us here like dogs!"

"Act like dogs, I'll treat you like dogs," J. C. said, turning and walking back toward the café.

Miss Bell was standing outside the door of the café watching.

"Is my steak done?" he asked, after he finished and walked up to where she was.

She laughed and nodded her pretty head as she turned and went inside. He followed.

"Welcome to Dallas, Texas, J. C. Holderfield. You're going to make quite a name for yourself."

"Who were they?" he asked.

"Two local troublemakers, Wade Sparks and Silas Cook. They work for Ike Booth."

After he left the café, he walked to the small, box-like hotel. A tall, thin, sickly-looking fellow stood behind a small counter.

"I need a room," J. C. told the man.

"You the new marshal?"

"I am; J. C. Holderfield is the name."

"I'm Eldon McElroy. Glad you're here. I saw what you done awhile ago. That was really something to see."

"You got a room?"

"Sure do, Mr. Holderfield. Room number one, right in front with a window; best room in the house."

"How much?"

"Dollar a night or five dollars a week. We change sheets once a week. Hot baths out back are fifty cents."

J. C. paid for a month, took the key, and went to his room.

Members of the town council were already there when he arrived at the big house on the hill at the edge of town. John Bryan himself opened the front door to J. C.'s knock.

"Come in, Marshal. We were just enjoying a laugh about the events of this afternoon. That was quite an introduction you gave everybody."

"Figured since we didn't have a jail yet, that was the only way to make my point."

"I'd say your point was well made," the storekeeper said, ushering him into a large den. Several others were sitting around the room; they all rose and offered handshakes.

Sam Pryor and John Bryan, of course, were there. Doctor James Bixby and Benjamin Cantrell, the lawyer, were introduced to him. Virgil Atkins, the undertaker was there. Reverend Brown and Jeb Sawyer, the sawmill operator rounded out the town council.

Sam Pryor introduced J. C. to each of them as they shook hands.

"Don't know how many of you witnessed the events that took place this afternoon," Sam Pryor told them, "But our new town marshal proved real quick that we need a jail."

"I'll put a crew to work on it come morning," Jeb Sawyer spoke up. "We can have one put up in a week."

"All in favor of us building a jail say *aye*," John Bryan said. A chorus of *aye's* sounded. "Anybody opposed?" he asked, but there was none.

"J. C. asked that we pass an ordinance making it against the law to carry a firearm in city limits, *and* that we post a sign on each end of town to that effect," Bryan told them. "I make a motion we do what he asked."

"I'll second it," Doctor Bixby said.

"All in favor say *aye*," Bryan said.

Again, everybody agreed.

"How long you plan on keeping Wade and Silas chained up out there?" Benjamin Cantrell, the lawyer, asked.

"Long as it takes," J. C. told them flatly.

"To do what?" the lawyer persisted.

"To convince lawbreakers there's a price to pay for breaking the law."

"Well," John Bryan said. "I think we can all agree we've hired ourselves the right man for the job."

It rained in Dallas, Texas that night.

J. C. lay in his room and listened to the pouring rain on the sheet iron roof. He thought about the two men chained to the water pump and smiled. He decided to keep them there for a couple of days and then turn them loose.

He had learned their names were Wade Sparks and Silas Cook and that they both worked for Ike Booth, the town troublemaker. Sam Pryor had warned J. C. that the saloon owner also had some real bad men on his payroll. One in particular was said to be the worst. His name was Bill Ivey; they called him *Poison Ivey!*

"He's a killer, J. C.," Pryor told him. "Watch out for him. They say he's killed a dozen men or more."

"Much obliged for the information," J. C. had told him.

As he lay there listening to the rain, his mind shifted to Opal Sullivan. Thinking about her brought a good feeling.

As he always did when he thought of Opal, he pulled the yellow ribbon from his pocket. He let it slowly slide through his fingers—remembering last time he saw her—remembering her promise to him and his to her.

Sure would like to see her again, he thought. *Maybe when things settle down here a bit, I might ride back to that ranch and see how she's doing—yeah, I might just do that. It couldn't be too far.*

With the memory of Opal and the soothing sound of rain on the roof, he drifted off to a deep sleep.

CHAPTER XIII

As was his custom, he woke before daylight, dressed, and washed up in the wash pan in his room. He checked his Colt and replaced it in its holster after assuring himself it was fully loaded.

On the way to the Dinner Bell Café, he stopped by to check on his two prisoners. They both were awake, drenched from the rain, shivering, and cursing him. He lifted a thin grin and continued toward the café.

Lamplight from inside the café cast a square pattern of light on the wet street outside the window. He pushed open the door and stepped inside.

Miss Bell stepped from the kitchen and greeted him with a happy smile.

"Good morning, J. C."

"Mornin', May Bell."

"You're up and around mighty early this morning; you're my first customer. Didn't you sleep well?"

"Yes, ma'am, I always sleep well. The rain on the roof helped, too. I always enjoy the rain."

"It was nice, wasn't it? I doubt Wade and Silas liked it though."

"They seemed pretty put out when I stopped by a minute ago. I'll take them some coffee and breakfast in a bit."

"I appreciate what you did yesterday."

"They had no call to do what they did."

"I'll bring you some coffee; ready for breakfast?"

"I'm always ready for breakfast."

She brought a pot of coffee and a cup and poured it full. "What would you like for breakfast?" she asked.

"Surprise me," he said, lifting a grin.

"I can do that," she said, laughing a pretty laugh. "I'm full of surprises. Just sit right there; I'm going to fill you up."

J. C. was blowing the steam away from his coffee when three, tough-looking men stalked into the café. They walked to his table and spread out around him. Their hands hovered only inches from their side arms.

"Boss wants to see you!" one of the men said curtly.

J. C. glanced up at the speaker, continuing to blow steam from his coffee.

"Who's *the boss?*"

The speaker cut an annoyed look at both of his companions and then back at J. C.

"Ike Booth, of course! Come with us!" he said loudly.

J. C. rose from his chair as if to go with them, but instead, stepped backwards away from them and let his hand rest on the handle of his Colt Dragoon.

"Tell your *boss* if he wants to see me, he knows where to find me. Now get out of my face—my coffee's getting cold."

His move took them by surprise. Shock swept across their faces. For a moment they froze in place, obviously knowing he had the advantage.

"One more thing," J. C. told them. "We've got a new law in Dallas against carrying firearms. I realize you didn't know about it yet so I'll let it slide this time, but next time I see you, don't be packing! Understand?"

Again, they exchanged glances.

"I *said, do you understand?*" he said, pushing the question from between clenched teeth.

They nodded and backed up a step or two before turning and hurrying from the café. He calmly sat back down and took a sip of coffee.

"I saw and heard it all," May Bell said from the doorway to the kitchen. "I can't believe they backed down like that! What would you have done if they called your bluff?"

"I would'a killed them."

It was her turn to be shocked—and she was. She nodded and went back into the kitchen.

After he finished his breakfast, he took coffee and two breakfasts out to the prisoners. They accepted what he brought and actually seemed grateful.

True to his word, Jeb Sawyer, the sawmill owner, arrived with his crew to begin work on the new jail. J. C. walked down the street to the lot where the jail would be built.

"Mornin', Marshal," Sawyer greeted.

"Mornin', Mr. Sawyer."

"After you left the meeting last night, the rest of us talked about the jail. We decided to build it outta logs to make it sturdier. They pretty well left the size up to me. I figured something like twelve by twenty, divided into two rooms—one for the actual jail and the other for an office. That sound about right?"

"Sounds good to me," J. C. agreed.

As they talked, two large log wagons pulled up loaded with peeled logs. A crew of six men went to work unloading the wagons.

"We outta have it finished in a few days," Sawyer told him.

"That'd be good," J. C. said. "Reckon I better go check on my prisoners. Much obliged for getting started so quick on the jail."

On his way back to the town square where the prisoners were, he decided he had made his point and would release them. They had already finished their breakfasts and were sitting on the ground with their backs against the rock water trough when he walked up.

"If you boys think you can behave yourselves, I've decided to turn you loose. Just so you'll know, we've got a new law in town against carrying firearms. You can pick up your guns down at the new jail in a few days, but don't wear them in town. Understand?"

They both nodded agreement. He took the keys from his pocket and unlocked the chains around their ankles. They climbed to their feet, brushed dirt from their britches, and headed for the saloon.

"Just you wait until *Poison Ivey* hears about your *new law—ain't* no way you're man enough to take *his* guns!" one of the men said over his shoulder as he walked away.

J. C. decided to make the rounds of all businesses in Dallas and introduce himself. Since he had already met many of them, he decided to visit only those he hadn't yet met.

His first stop was at *Sosa's Gun & Saddle Shop.* It was a small, slat-board building next door to the livery stable. He opened the front door and stepped inside. The smallish, Mexican fellow who swung a look at him was short, clean shaven, and had salt and pepper hair. He wore a denim apron and was seated at a wooden work bench with a leather saddle across it.

"Can I help you, senor?" the man asked with a broken Mexican accent.

"I'm J. C. Holderfield; I'm the new town marshal. I just wanted to stop by and introduce myself."

The saddlemaker rose from his workbench and stuck out his hand.

"I'm *Armando Sosa.* Everybody in Dallas has already heard of you. It is good to meet you."

"I've never met a gunsmith and saddlemaker before," J. C. told him.

"My family has been gunsmiths and saddlemakers for generations. My father and his father before him were all gunsmiths. It's all I have ever known."

J. C. swung a look around the small shop. Several finished saddles hung on short ropes from the ceiling, along with bridles, leather saddlebags, and even an assortment of beautiful leather belts and gun holsters. A glass case held an assortment of guns of all kinds and makes.

"Looks like you do good work," J. C. said, admiring the craftsmanship of the items displayed. "You ever work on a Colt Dragoon?"

He drew his gun and handed it to the gunsmith.

The man examined it carefully, unloading it and looking long at the internal workings of the weapon before answering.

"No, senor, this is a beautiful weapon. This is the first I have seen. It must be brand new."

"Actually, I doubt it's even on the market yet. I think the only ones distributed so far have been to the army."

"Very interesting," the gunsmith said. "Very interesting. If I can ever help you, Marshal, just let me know."

"Do you have a holster that would fit my Colt Dragoon?" he asked.

"If I don't, I can make one. Could you leave it with me for a few days? Stop back by in a few days and I'll have one for you."

"I will, much obliged. I've got another I can use until then."

He left the shop and continued on up the street. His next stop was at the *Cedar Snag,* the town's newspaper. He opened the door and stepped inside.

A man with a green visor above his eyes looked up from a desk.

"Howdy," J. C. greeted. "I'm J. C. Holderfield, the new town marshal."

"Yes—yes, indeed, Mr. Holderfield. I'm Frank Bridges. I was just setting type for a story about you. It's a real pleasure to meet you."

"What kind of story?"

"It's all about how you arrested two of our local troublemakers after they molested Miss Preston over at the café and how you chained them to the water fountain in the town square. It will make quite a story."

"How long you been in Dallas, Mr. Bridges?"

"We just opened our newspaper two months ago."

"I see. Well, I was just trying to get around and meet all of our merchants. I'll be anxious to read your story."

"The paper will be out in a couple of days. I understand we're building a new jail, too?"

"Yep."

"Dallas is growing. Maybe since you're here, it will grow even faster."

"We'll see, Mr. Bridges, we'll see. Good day to you."

After he left the newspaper office, he stopped by the general store to see John Bryan.

"Morning, Marshal," the storekeeper greeted.

"Mornin', John. I was just kinda making the rounds meeting all the merchants today."

"That's good. I saw you release Wade and Silas awhile ago."

"Yeah, figured I made my point—weren't no use keeping them chained up any longer."

While he talked, he spotted a stack of western hats on a shelf against the wall.

"Got one of them hats in my size?" he asked. "This old coonskin cap is about to come apart on me."

"Bet I do, let's take a look-see."

Bryan walked over to the shelf and looked through the hats. He selected a pretty brown one and a flat-brimmed black one and handed them to J. C.

"Try one of these on for size."

J. C. swiped the coonskin cap from his head and carefully set the flat, wide-brimmed hat on his head. It fit perfectly.

"I think it's time I wore something besides these deerskin britches and top, too."

"Take a look at these black business suits I just got in. One of those and a white shirt would look good on you."

He decided John was right. He bought the suit, two white shirts, a black string tie, and both the black and brown hats.

"How much?"

"It all comes to sixty dollars."

J. C. fished the money from his pocket and paid him.

"It'll look good on you, J. C., you'll look more like a lawman."

"Well, reckon I need all the help I can get," he said, turning toward the door. He left the store feeling good.

He walked back to where the crew was building the jail. He was amazed how much progress they had made just in half a day. All four walls were waist high already.

After he left the jailhouse site, he went to the livery, saddled Blackie, and rode a quarter mile circle around Dallas to get familiar with the surroundings. He ended up on a high bluff outside town overlooking the Trinity River.

He was told the Trinity flowed over seven hundred miles, all within the Texas border. It had four tributaries and was a barrier that restricted crossing at most points. The crossing just outside Dallas was the only crossing for a hundred miles.

As sundown faded and twilight settled, he rode back to town and put Blackie away. Full dark had shrouded the streets. The four coal oil lanterns that lit the street painted yellowish circles of light along the dark street. Most businesses had long since closed—only the saloon, hotel, and the Dinner Bell Café had lights showing. He headed for the café.

Halfway there, the night was shattered by a gunshot from the direction of the saloon. J. C. broke into a trot and headed that way. He stopped abruptly just outside the batwing doors and looked over them.

A tall, thin fellow stood gazing down at a man on the floor. A thin tendril of blue gun smoke snaked upward from the nose of the Paterson .36 in his hand. Several onlookers stared down at the man on the floor.

J. C. lifted his Colt Dragoon from its holster, thumbed back the hammer, and stepped inside.

"Drop the gun!" he said firmly.

The thin gunman twisted a look at him, but continued to hold the smoking gun. The man was tall, thin, and had a pointed chin. His face was pock-marked and his eyes were pale grey.

"I won't say it again!" J. C. said, this time louder and firmer.

The thin fellow paused another moment before spinning the gun into his holster.

"Who are you?" the shooter asked sarcastically.

"I'm the new town marshal; Holderfield is the name—J. C. Holderfield."

He walked slowly and carefully toward the man on the floor, but kept the Colt in his hand.

"What happened here?" J. C. asked.

"This fellow called me a card cheat; I called him a liar. He braced me; I killed him—end of story."

"Anybody see it different?" J. C. asked, glancing slowly around the room. Every man was shaking his head, agreeing with the shooter's version.

"What's your name?"

"I'm *Bill Ivey!*" the man said proudly, like it was a name of some importance. "Some call me *Poison Ivey.*"

"Well, Mr. Ivey, I'm afraid I'm gonna have to ask for your gun. It's against the law to carry a firearm in the city limits."

"My gun?—over my dead body! *Nobody* takes *Poison Ivey's* gun!—nobody!"

"Well, Mr. Ivey, I hope it won't come to that, but that's a choice you gotta make. Hand it over or draw it, whatever suits you, but if you draw it I'll kill you where you stand."

The gunman looked confused. He jerked nervous looks around the room and then back at J. C.

"But—but you already got your gun out, that ain't fair!" he protested.

"You're old enough to know life ain't always *fair*. Now draw it or lift it out with two fingers real easy like. *I won't say it again!*"

J. C. knew when a rattlesnake is cornered it's impossible to predict what they will do. With his Dragoon out, pointed squarely at the gunman and with the hammer already cocked, no matter how fast the gunman was, he didn't stand a chance—and Bill Ivey knew it. That's why he ate crow and slowly, carefully, lifted his pistol from its holster and dropped it on the floor.

"Good choice. Now turn around and put your hands on top of your head!"

The gunman did as he was told. J. C. reached down, picked up the pistol, and jammed it behind his belt buckle.

"Which one of you is Ike Booth?" J. C. asked loudly. A heavy man with thin hair on top of his head and a mustache on his top lip stepped forward. He was well-dressed in a black business suit and white shirt. A string tie hung down the front of his shirt. His coat was open in front and J. C. could see he was unarmed.

"I'm Ike Booth."

"I understand you wanted to see me?"

"Another time, Marshal," the man said firmly. "Another time."

"Whatever suits you, Mr. Booth. You know where to find me."

"Indeed I do."

J. C. poked the shooter's back with the nose of his Colt Dragoon.

"Let's go, Mr. Ivey. You're under arrest for carrying a firearm in town limits."

"You'll pay for this!" the gunman said loudly. "This ain't over by a long shot!"

"Careful, Mr. Ivey. Threatening a law officer is a serious offense. That alone could get you ten days chained in the town square."

"You wouldn't dare!"

"You might be surprised what I might do. Now move!"

J. C. marched the gunman to the water trough in the town square and locked a chain around the gunman's ankle. He stuck the key in his pocket, turned, and gazed up at the sky.

"Sure looks like it might rain. Have a good evening, Mr. Ivey," he said over his shoulder as he turned and walked away.

Word of the arrest of the gunman, *Poison Ivey,* spread through Dallas like wildfire. Suddenly there wasn't a gun in sight anywhere in town limits.

For the next several days, visitors who rode into Dallas and saw the signs at both ends of town, and then saw the man chained to the water pump in the town square, would ask somebody why he was there. When they learned about the consequences of wearing a gun in the town limits, they usually unbuckled their guns and left them in their saddlebags as soon as they tied their mounts to the hitching rails.

Once in awhile, there was an exception.

His name was Utah Swan. J. C. saw him when he rode his chestnut sorrel down the street past the hotel and reined up in front of the saloon. He could tell by the looks of the man what he was—he had seen his kind before. He was a hard man, hard and mean and the kind of man who didn't like rules—he lived by his *own* rules. J. C. saw him and knew he was trouble waiting to happen.

J. C. stepped off the porch in front of the hotel and approached the newcomer. The man swung to the ground, tied his chestnut to the hitching rail, and headed toward the front door of the saloon.

"Hold up there, stranger," J. C. said. "Reckon you didn't see the sign at the edge of town. It's against the law to wear a gun in Dallas, Texas. I'll ask you to unbuckle it and leave it in your saddlebags."

The man paused and swung an annoyed look over his shoulder.

"Look, *sonny!* I've rode a long way. I'm bone tired and thirsty. I'm going into that saloon and have a drink! Now get outta my sight before you annoy me and make me mad—and you don't wanna make me mad."

"No, sir, I surely don't, and you're shore welcome to go have your drink, just as soon as you unbuckle that gun belt."

The man stopped in his tracks and stood motionless for a long moment. J. C. thought he was going to take off his gun, but just in case he chose otherwise, J. C. lifted his Dragoon from its holster, thumbed back the hammer, and held it beside his right leg.

The stranger turned to face J. C. and dropped into a *gunfighter stance.*

His knees were slightly bent, his body squarely facing J. C. His hand hung only a hair's breadth from the hickory butt of his .36 caliber Paterson revolver.

That's when the gunfighter saw J. C.'s big revolver in his hand hanging by his leg. His eyes went wide with surprise.

"What's your name, Mister?" J. C. asked.

"I'm Utah Swan! What's it to you?"

"Just wanted to know what name to put on your grave marker, that's all," he said calmly.

A crowd had emerged from the saloon and spread along the front, well out of the line of fire. Others had stepped from buildings along the street. They all heard the exchange.

"Maybe you don't know *who* I am," the man shouted. "I'm *Utah Swan!* I'm the fastest gunny in the southwest. Do you *really* think I'm gonna give my gun up to some two-bit law-dog from a hick town in Texas? I can put a bullet in you even before you can raise your gun and fire."

"Maybe," J. C. said casually, forcing the words between clenched teeth. "But are you willing to bet your life on it? It's your choice—either unbuckle it or use it, and right now I don't much care which."

It was clear from the man's face that J. C.'s words had shaken the gunman's confidence. A confused look swept across his face. He hesitated for a moment. J. C.'s unwavering gaze fixed on the man's eyes.

He saw the gunfighter's eyes squint and knew he was about to draw. In half a heartbeat, the gunfighter's hand dipped to the butt of his pistol. The gun leaped from its holster and suddenly stopped midway to level. Utah Swan's eyes bugged wide. His mouth dropped open in disbelief. He was staring at the nose of a big Colt Dragoon .44 Revolver—the most powerful handgun in the world.

It took a split instant for the gunfighter to recover from the shock of being beaten so badly.

"How—how'd you do that?" the gunfighter asked. "Nobody's ever beat me! Nobody!"

"Never was a man that couldn't be beat," J. C. told him. "Now are you gonna drop it or die where you stand?"

He dropped it.

"Good choice. Now you can go have your drink."

He kept the gunman, *Poison Ivey,* chained in the town square three days before releasing him.

"This ain't over by a long shot," the gunman told J. C. as he walked away. "Next time, I'll kill you!"

"Anytime, anyplace," J. C. told him.

CHAPTER XIV

Less than two weeks after beginning the project, the sawmill crew completed the new jail and office. J. C. purchased an iron cot and mattress from the store and moved from the hotel to the office. He liked his new home. It was sturdy, laid out well, and smelled of fresh-cut timber.

John Bryan told him the town council was very pleased with his progress toward cleaning up Dallas. "Folks feel comfortable walking down the street now."

"Much obliged," J. C. said. "Don't know what Ike Booth's up to yet, but I figure he'll make his move soon."

"A word to the wise; I'd watch my back if I was you."

The councilman's advice became prophetic that very night. J. C.'s custom was to make his rounds of all the businesses before retiring for the night. It was late. Every business had long since closed except for saloon. Three horses stood hip-shod in front, tied to the hitching rail; otherwise, the streets of Dallas were deserted.

He walked slowly, cautiously examining every doorway, every alleyway, every place a man could hide, waiting to do him harm. He shook the front door of each business to make sure they were securely locked before moving on up the street.

The night was quiet—still—uncomfortable; even the piano in the saloon had fallen silent. The flickering light from the four street lanterns cast eerie, dancing shadows in the dusty street.

The sound of his own footsteps on the wooden boardwalk seemed unusually loud in the deathly quietness. A black cat suddenly burst from underneath the wooden boardwalk and scampered away. It suddenly dawned on him that he had drawn his Colt Dragoon, raked back the hammer, and had it trained on the cat without even realizing it.

I'm getting jumpy. But better to be jumpy than dead, I reckon. I know Ike Booth's gonna send his men after me sooner or later; it's just a matter of time. Maybe I need to force the issue a bit. I don't like this waiting around for something to happen, not knowing what or when.

He twisted around to watch the black cat disappear into the night—that just might have saved his life. A blast from atop a building across the street shattered a store window exactly where his head would have been had he not twisted around to look at the retreating cat. His head shot upward in time to see the fiery afterglow of the rifle. He snapped off a shot in that direction even as he bent from the waist and raced across the street toward the building from which the shooter fired—it was Bryan's General Store.

Four buildings were all tied together with no separation between them. With his Colt Dragoon in his hand, he raced around the end of the last building, down the length of it, and stopped before rounding the final corner. He chanced a quick look.

The vague silhouette of a man was halfway down a ladder that leaned against the back wall of the general store. He lifted the Colt Dragoon and fired.

The loud blast of the powerful gun shredded the stillness of the night. He saw the figure pitch over backward off the ladder. J. C. raced around the corner and the short distance to where the man lay. A rifle lay nearby—he kicked it away.

Running footsteps sounded behind him, coming fast. He whirled with his gun ready for action. A man carrying a lighted lantern came hurrying up.

"Don't shoot, Marshal!" a man's voice shouted. "It is *Armando Sosa*. I heard the shooting and come to see if I could help."

"Somebody tried to bushwhack me from the roof of the store. Bring that light over and let's see who it is."

They looked down into the lifeless face of Silas Cook, one of Ike Booth's men.

"Appears you've made some enemies, Marshal," the saddle-maker said.

"Seems so. Help me carry him down to the undertaker's office, will you?"

After they turned the body over to Virgil Atkins, J. C. went back to his office, unbuckled his gun and put it underneath his pillow, pried off his boots, and flopped down on the cot.

Reckon it's time to have a visit with Ike Booth, he decided, just before he drifted off to sleep.

The undertaker buried Silas Cook the following morning. Except for the undertaker, not another living person attended the burying.

J. C. received a stack of wanted posters in the mail and spent an hour or so looking through them. One jumped out at him immediately—it was none other than Bill "Poison" Ivey. It seems he was wanted up in Missouri for murder and bank robbery. There was a three hundred dollar reward on him, dead or alive. J. C. folded the poster and stuck it in his pocket. Someone had told him the day before that Ivey was hanging out down in Shanty Town.

He decided it was time to pay a visit to the notorious community. He walked to the livery, saddled Blackie, and rode the quarter mile to the crude collection of ramshackled slat-board shacks.

The street was no more than a good stone's throw in length. As he rode slowly between the twin rows of buildings, a collection of raggedly dressed men and hollow-eyed women watched him with suspicion.

The largest building along the street had a crude, painted sign identifying it as the saloon. He reined up in front of it, stepped slowly to the ground, and tied his gelding to the hitching rail.

He lifted his Colt Dragoon, checked to make sure it was fully loaded, and settled it gently back into the leather holster.

There was no boardwalk. He stepped directly from the dusty ground through an open door into the room. The place looked and smelled more like a pigsty than a saloon. The stench of vomit, stale whisky, and unwashed bodies was enough to turn one's stomach.

The room was small, no more than twelve feet square. It had a hard-packed dirt floor that was slick from spilt whisky and vomit. There was no light except that which filtered in through the open door.

A heavyset, Mexican bartender lifted a look from his folded arms as J. C. stepped through the door. Two other men sat at a rickety table. Both men wore guns.

J. C. walked over to the table and looked down at them. One of them had a pale look on his face.

"Something bothering you, mister? Looks like you saw a ghost just now."

"Just surprised to see a lawman in Shanty Town, that's all."

"You a wanted man?"

"No."

"I notice both of you are packing guns. That's against the law. That's five days in jail right there. You wanna spend five days in our new jail?"

The man looked straight at him and shook his head. "Tell you what—I'll forget about the five days in jail if you tell me where I can find a fellow that calls himself *Poison Ivey.* What'll it be?"

"Never heard of him," the man said nervously, glancing quickly at the bartender.

"Then get on your feet! You're under arrest for carrying a gun."

The man wet his dry lips. Sweat suddenly appeared on his face. His eyes rounded.

"Okay, okay! He's with a girl called *Texas Rose*— little shack across the street."

Without a word, J. C. turned and left the saloon.

Half way across the street he met a young Mexican boy who looked to be twelve or so. He was barefooted and wore dirty, tattered clothes. J. C. pulled a dollar from his pocket and held it out to the boy.

"Texas Rose—where is she?"

The boy reached a dirty hand and grabbed the silver dollar with one hand and pointed to a small shack.

J. C. nodded his *thanks* and headed toward the building the boy had indicated. He stopped just outside the slat-board door, pulled his Colt Dragoon, raked back the hammer and kicked the door down.

A man and woman jerked a surprised look from a pallet on the dirt floor—the man was Bill *Poison* Ivey. He lunged for a pistol lying nearby, grabbed it, and lifted it toward the marshal—he didn't make it.

A well-placed shot buried in the gunman's chest. He slumped back on the dirty pallet. The woman screamed. The sound of J. C.'s shot reverberated along the street.

After the shooting of the murderer, Bill Ivey, things quieted down in Dallas, Texas—at least until the morning of June 18, 1848.

"GOLD!" a stranger shouted, running along the street.. . . . "They discovered GOLD in California!"

Within short hours, adventurous men abandoned whatever they were doing, saddled a horse or hurriedly threw a few supplies into a wagon, and set out on a two-thousand mile trip clear across the country to the gold fields of California—the gold rush was on!

Ike Booth, along with his henchmen, joined those who left. Shanty Town was abandoned, and Dallas, Texas was transformed overnight into a quiet, peaceful, small town.

J. C. hired Jeb Sawyer and his sawmill crew to build him a four-room log cabin on a lot at the edge of town. It took them five weeks to complete the job. They also built sturdy furniture and furnished it. When it was finished, J.

C. stood in front of it and gazed at the first real home he had known since he was eleven years old.

For several weeks he hadn't been able to get Opal Sullivan off his mind and finally admitted to himself that she was the *real* reason he had decided to build his cabin.

The following day, he rented a buggy from the livery, dressed in his black business suit, white shirt, string tie, and flat-brimmed hat, and headed north. He figured it wasn't more than a hard day's drive to Sod Horton's ranch where he had left Opal—he had to know—he had to know if she had waited for him and still loved him.

He left at well before first light and followed the river northwest until late afternoon. Up ahead he saw the area know as the *grasslands.* He remembered passing through it when he left the Horton Ranch with Capt. Walker and the other Rangers. It was a well-watered, grass prairieland that stretched for a hundred miles. It was the perfect place to raise cattle—he knew he was getting close and he was getting nervous.

What if she's not there? What if she's met someone else and fallen in love with them?—after all, it had been close to four years.

Up ahead and off to the left, he spotted a large herd of cattle grazing peacefully on the knee-high grass. Off in the shimmering distance the vague outline of several buildings took shape.

That would be Sod Horton's ranch, he thought.

He pulled his team of horses to a stop and climbed down from the buggy. He carefully brushed the dust from his suit coat and vest. He struck his black, flat-brimmed hat against his leg several times to rid it of the excess dust.

As he stood there staring at the distant ranch buildings and thinking, his hand reached to his vest pocket and withdrew the frayed, yellow ribbon. For a long minute he stared at it. Hot, wet tears escaped from his eyes. He swiped them away with the back of his hand, climbed back into the buggy, and popped the reins. His team moved forward toward the ranch.

CHAPTER XV

While still a ways from the ranch, three riders suddenly appeared. They separated as they approached and surrounded him. They all carried long rifles in their hands.

"This is Horton property," one of the riders said, watching him closely. "Who are you and why are you here?"

"I'm J. C. Holderfield. I visited the Hortons a few years ago and left a friend of mine with them; Opal Sullivan. I've come to check on her. Do you know if she's still here?"

"She's here. We'll escort you in."

The speaker turned his mount and led the way. The remaining two riders fell in behind him, but stayed too far back for him to inquire further about Opal.

The sprawling ranch was pretty much as he remembered it, except it appeared they had added several more barns and another bunkhouse.

A whiskered old stableman walked from a barn and took charge of his team as he stepped from the buggy. Sod Horton appeared at the front door of the big house and walked to meet him. He didn't seem to have aged a single day in the last four years. He had a questioning look on his face as he drew near, like he didn't recognize him.

"I'm Sod Horton," he said, extending a welcoming hand and lingering a look on the badge pinned on J. C.'s black vest. "You look vaguely familiar, but—? "

"J. C. Holderfield, Mr. Horton. I was here a few years ago with Sam Walker."

"Why, of course! I should have remembered, but my memory ain't what it used to be. Let's see, that's been three, maybe four years. You've grown up considerable since then. How is Sam?"

"I'm sorry, Mr. Horton, but Sam was killed at the battle of *Huamantla, Mexico* October 9th, 1847."

A sad look swept over the rancher's rugged face. He dropped his gaze and was silent for a long minute.

"Sam Walker was a good man, most likely one of the best I've ever known. I'll miss him."

"Yes, sir, he was. I figure folks will talk about Sam Walker for a long time after most of us are gone."

The rancher nodded agreement.

"Come on in the house. Evelyn will have the coffee hot, as usual. So you're a lawman now?" the rancher asked as they walked toward the house.

"Yes, sir, I'm the town marshal over in Dallas."
"Dallas, huh? Never been there myself, but from the way my men talk about it, sounds like they needed one."

" Is—how's Miss Sullivan doing?"

"Opal? She's fine. Doubt you'd recognize her though, she's grown into a beautiful, young lady. Kinda figured that's why you're here."

The front door suddenly flew open and she was there!

Horton was right; he wouldn't have recognized her in a million years! She had on a light blue, floor-length dress. Her long, blonde hair hung in curls about her shoulders. Her jade-green eyes sparkled in the evening sunlight and were rounded with shocked surprise.

"J. C.?" she screamed through a mixture of sobs and happy laughter, breaking into a run. He matched her step-for-step as they raced toward one another, finally folding into each other's open arms.

For a long moment they held each other tightly. Hot tears wet his neck. He buried his face in her neck and smelled the special scent he had remembered all these years that was her—just her.

He felt her fingers clawing for a tighter hold, clinging to him, grasping, as if she would never again let him go. He pulled her even closer.

"It's been so long," she whispered through choking sobs, "but I knew you'd come."

"I promised I would," were the only words his emotions would allow him speak.

When the embrace finally ended, they discovered Evelyn Horton had joined her husband. Both stood by quietly as J. C. and Opal had their reunion.

"Not a day went by that she didn't speak of you," the rancher's wife told him. "She almost put her eyes out looking down the road, watching for you."

"Sorry it took so long," he said, twisting a blurry look at Opal.

"You're here now and that's all that matters," she said, hugging him again.

"J. C. told me that our friend, Sam Walker, was killed in the war," the rancher told his wife, as they all headed into the house.

"Oh, Sod, I'm so sorry. I know how much you thought of him."

"Yes—yes, he was a dear friend. J. C.'s a lawman now. He's the marshal over in Dallas."

"And a handsome one, too," Opal said, gazing up at him.

"You-all go on into the den," Evelyn told them. "I'll bring coffee."

J. C. and Opal sat down on a large, cowhide-covered sofa. Sod Horton folded into an overstuffed chair.

"Didn't you join up with Sam and the Texas Rangers when you left?" the rancher asked.

"Yes, sir, we fought with Zachary Taylor all through the war."

"Thought so. We got bits and pieces of the news from the war, but it's hard to get much news about much of anything way out here."

"Well, we won," J. C. said. "That's the important thing. Hope that ends it. War ain't pretty."

"You planning on staying in law work?" Horton asked.

"That depends. I like the work, *and* it's a living."

"Is it dangerous?" Opal asked.

"Living is dangerous now days," J. C. told her.

"That's a fact," the rancher agreed. "How long can you stay with us, J. C.?"

"I need to leave at first light."

He glanced quickly at Opal. He saw a frightened look sweep across her face. A tear glistened in the corner of both eyes.

"Is there someplace I could talk with Opal alone?" he asked quickly.

"Of course," the rancher said, pushing up from his chair. "Evelyn and I will leave you two alone. I should have realized you needed to talk."

The rancher met his wife as she was bringing coffee and motioned for her to go with him. She nodded understanding.

When they were alone, he looked deep into her eyes; they looked sad, disappointed, frightened.

He took her hands in his and squeezed them.

"Opal, I've thought of nothing but you ever since I left. I've grown to realize how much I love you and want to spend the rest of my life with you. I want you to be my wife, if you'll have me?"

Her eyes suddenly rounded and her mouth flew open. She lunged forward, wrapping her arms around his neck and pulling him to her. It seemed she could hold back the flood of tears no longer. Through happy, choking sobs, the words poured out.

"If *I'll have you?* I've thought of nothing else since the first day I met you! Oh, yes! Yes, I'll marry you! That would make me the happiest woman in the whole world!"

He pulled her to him. Their lips sought and found one another in a kiss that was four years in the making.

After a bit, they went looking for the Hortons and shared the happy news.

"I just couldn't be happier," Evelyn Horton exclaimed. "Opal coming here was an answer to prayer. She has become the daughter I was never able to give my husband."

Mrs. Horton and Opal shared a long hug.

"Say you young folks are leaving in the morning?" Sod Horton asked.

"That's our plans, yes, sir," J. C. said.

"Then we need to celebrate tonight! Evelyn, tell the cook to prepare a wedding dinner! We're gonna celebrate our *daughter* getting married to a fine, young man!"

A hint of rosy sky peeked over the eastern horizon. J. C.'s buggy and team stood waiting, swatting pesky flies with their long tails.

Sod and Evelyn Horton stood with Opal and J. C.

"We're going to miss you," Mrs. Horton told Opal, wrapping her in a long hug.

"I'll miss you, too," Opal said sadly. "I appreciate everything both of you have done for me."

J. C stuck out a gloved hand to the big rancher. "I'm indebted to you, Mr. Horton. If there's ever anything I can do for you, just let me know."

"No, son, it's us that owe *you*. Take good care of our daughter."

"I will. That's a promise."

He assisted Opal as she climbed into the buggy seat. J. C. climbed in beside her and unwound the long reins from around the brake lever. He threaded the reins between his fingers and popped the rumps of the matched team. They moved forward. Opal scooted over in the middle of the seat against him.

Both J. C. and Opal twisted a look over their shoulder and lifted a wave *goodbye.*

Opal Sullivan and J. C. Holderfield were married two days later in the small church in Dallas, Texas. Reverend Brown performed the ceremony. More than half of the residents of Dallas were in attendance.

They set up housekeeping in their new log cabin at the edge of town. Opal delighted in fixing up their new home. She purchased cloth from the store and made curtains and a table cover, bought pots and pans for the kitchen, and crocheted a rug for their bedroom. It was a happy time.

Weeks passed quickly. Dallas was growing rapidly— new folks were moving in almost daily. The town council seemed happy with the job he was doing; in fact, they authorized him to hire a deputy to relieve him of some of the day-to-day, routine jobs.

He decided on a local man named Del Fisher. Del was older than J. C. by several years and had been up and down the trail enough to take care of himself. He felt Del would be loyal and could be counted on in whatever situation should arise.

He still had the usual drunks and Saturday night fights in the saloon, but rarely had anyone challenge his *no guns in the city limits* ordinance.

All that changed dramatically as a result of an article Frank Bridges wrote for his newspaper, the *Cedar Snag.*

The article was all about J. C. and his encounter with the gunman, *Poison Ivey,* and his supposed *gang.* The article, of course, bore little resemblance to the actual facts. It portrayed J. C. as being lightning fast with his Colt Dragoon .44 revolver and the toughest lawman in Texas. It made him out to be a hero who rescued the lady-folk of Dallas from the notorious bad men at the risk of his own life.

Somehow, the article from the small-town newspaper found its way into the hands of a writer from back east who wrote a dime novel about J. C. Holderfield and his "exploits." The book was entitled *"The Town Tamer."*

The book somehow found its way back into the newspaper man's hands and he rushed to proudly bring it to J. C. At first, J. C. laughed. He looked at the cover that showed a lawman standing on the street facing a whole gang of desperadoes single-handedly.

He took a few minutes to glance quickly through the thin book.

"This book is being read all over the country!" the newspaper man said proudly. "This book will make you famous, Marshal! Isn't this wonderful?"

"But Frank, that's not how it happened!"

"That don't matter," the newsman told him, shaking the thin little book in the air. "This is what folks will believe."

"I don't cotton to somebody telling something about me that ain't so."

After the newsman left, leaving the book on his desk, J. C. stared at it and thought about the unearned reputation the book might attach to him and what it could mean.

Having a reputation, deserved or not, could be a two-edged sword, he decided. *On one hand, it might prevent some from going up against me when I try to enforce the law.*

But on the other hand, some crave a reputation and are willing to risk their life to get it. Sure as shootin', there's gonna be some come looking for me so they can brag, "I'm the man that gunned down J. C. Holderfield, the fastest gunman in Texas."

Truth is, I know I'm not that fast. And if I'm gonna survive, I've got to be smarter than they are—I've got to figure out some advantage.

Passing the gunsmith shop, he turned in.

"Aw, *senor*. I think you forget about your gun, it's been so long."

"No, just been kinda busy."

"I have something to show you," the gunsmith said proudly. "A thought come to me during the night. I tried it and it worked."

"What do you mean?"

The gunsmith withdrew J. C.'s Colt Dragoon from the case and handed it to him. It didn't even resemble the gun he left with the gunsmith several weeks earlier. This one had white, bone handles with a coiled, black rattlesnake carved in the handles.

"I named it *The Rattler*," the gunsmith said.

"It's beautiful!" J. C. told him, turning the gun over and over in his hand.

"That is not the best part," the gunsmith told him, beaming proudly. "I made some changes inside the gun. It is empty; pull the hammer back until it locks in place and I'll show you what I mean."

J. C. did as the man said and heard a metallic click when the hammer locked in place.

"The trigger is what I call a *hair trigger*. You don't have to pull it, just touch it lightly."

J. C. feathered the trigger. The hammer slammed down and then immediately sprang back to the firing position, ready to fire again.

J. C. was shocked.

"What happened?" he asked, puzzled at the action.

"Try it again," the gunsmith said. "This time, pull the trigger again and again as fast as you can."

He did. Six times he feathered the trigger. Each time the hammer slammed forward and bounced back to the firing position as fast as he could pull the trigger. He couldn't believe what he just saw.

"I can't believe it!" he told the beaming gunsmith. "I've never seen anything like it!"

"There *isn't* anything like it, *senor*. This is the only one in existence. I installed a special spring mechanism. Once the hammer is pulled back and locked in full cocked position, it will fire and return to the firing position as fast as you can pull the trigger.

"With this gun, you can get off six shots in the same time most others can fire twice."

"It's amazing!" J. C. told him. "You've really hit on something."

"I hope you like it. I made it especially for you. I will never make another."

"Like it! I love it!"

Try as he would, the gunsmith refused to accept payment for the gun, but agreed to let J. C. pay for the matching black gun belt and holster.

He buckled it on, tied the leg strap, and slipped the beautiful *Rattler* into its new home.

As he left the gun shop, he determined to spend at least an hour each day practicing with his new gun. After supper, he went behind his house, unloaded his pistol, and spent almost two hours drawing it over and over and over again. By the end of the third week of practice, he could tell his speed had improved dramatically.

Del Fisher was working out well as J. C.'s deputy town marshal. He was a single man so he slept on the cot in the office and kept an eye on any prisoners.

Opal seemed to delight in married life. She was constantly finding new ways to make their house a home. She was a good cook and always had a meal prepared when J. C. got home in the evening.

John Bryan began drinking heavily and lost respectability in the community. Alexander Cockrell and his family moved to Dallas shortly after J. C. arrived in 1849. He ended up buying John Bryan out and started several other new businesses as well. He opened a new sawmill and lumber yard, a grist mill, and freighting business—Dallas was prospering.

A stage line opened a route through Dallas in 1851, connecting it with Austin, San Antonio, and Houston.

Opal announced that she was expecting, and a little girl was born on July 12, 1851. They named their daughter *Molly*. She proved to be a feisty little girl whose curiosity was unbounded.

In late August of that year a stranger rode into town on a high-stepping buckskin. Del Fisher saw him as he rode down the street and hurried to tell J. C.

"A stranger just rode into town and tied up at the saloon. I've seen his kind before. He's a gunfighter if I ever saw one. Thought you'd want to know."

"Was he wearing a gun?" J. C. asked.

"Yep, real fancy one all tied down and everything."

"Most likely just passing through," J. C. said. "But reckon we ought to go check it out."

He shrugged into his black, long-tailed suit jacket and took down his black, flat-brimmed hat from a wall peg and set it in place.

Together they walked up the street to the saloon. J. C. paused at the bat-wing doors and looked inside. Sure enough, the stranger stood at the bar with one foot on the brass railing, sipping a fresh drink in his right hand.

J. C. lifted his Dragoon slightly, settled it gently back into the black leather holster, and pushed through the doors. Del entered behind him and angled right, taking up a position behind the stranger. J. C. walked slowly, his gaze fixed upon the stranger, taking his measure.
He was average height, slim, and young, most likely barely out of his teens, if that. He wore his gun and

holster low on his right leg and tied just above his knee. It appeared to be one of the newer model Colt Dragoons.

The gunfighter flicked a side-ways glance as J. C. stopped in front of the bar six feet from the man.

"Just ride in?" J. C. asked.

The gunfighter twisted a look.

"Yep."

"Then maybe you missed the sign at the edge of town saying we don't allow guns in town limits."

"Reckon I must have," he said, taking a casual swallow of his drink. "I don't pay much attention to signs."

"Planning on staying in Dallas long?"

"Just long enough to do what I came here to do."

"And what would that be?"

"Are you J. C. Holderfield?"

"I am."

"You're the one they're calling the *fastest gun in Texas* ain't you?"

"I've been called a lot of things. What do they call you?"

"I'm Trey Booker, from Missouri. Maybe you've heard of me."

"'Fraid not, but I'll have to ask you to unbuckle your gun belt, Mr. Booker. You can pick it up at the marshal's office when you leave town."

"Not likely. I don't give up my gun to *nobody.*"

"Then we've got ourselves a real problem here, Mr. Booker, 'cause, you see, you're breaking the law by wearing your gun in town. You're either gonna pull that gun off or I'm gonna have to arrest you and take you to jail."

As he spoke, J. C. brushed back the edge of his black suit jacket behind the butt of his Dragoon and rested his hand on the gun's handle.

"It's your choice," he said in a voice that was suddenly firm and cold.

All talk by the other customers in the saloon ceased at the marshal's words. For a long, tense moment the room was deathly silent.

J. C. watched the gunfighter carefully, alert for any sign of what he would do. The man who called himself *Booker* swallowed the remainder of his whisky in one gulp and slowly, deliberately, set his glass on the bar. He removed his foot from the brass foot rail, and turned to face the marshal. His right hand hung loosely by his side, only a hair's breadth from the butt of his gun.

His cold, grey eyes flicked from the marshal's hard stare to his hand that rested on the handle of his Colt Dragoon.

"You've got me at a disadvantage, Marshal. It wouldn't be a *fair* fight."

"I don't fight *fair*. I fight to win, that's why I'm still alive. Talkin's over. You got exactly three heartbeats to unbuckle that gun or use it. I won't be tellin' you again."

A sudden helpless, almost frantic look swept over the gunfighter's face.

"But—but this ain't the way it was supposed to be!" he protested in a quivering, almost *pleading* voice.

While he was protesting, Del walked up behind him with his gun drawn and cocked. He stuck the nose of his pistol against the gunfighter's back and lifted the gun from the stranger's holster with his free hand.

"Let's go," the deputy told the gunfighter.

"But—but this ain't fair!"

"Tell it to the judge," Del told him, shoving him toward the door.

J. C. followed behind his deputy as he marched the gunfighter down the street to the jail. He shoved him inside and locked the barred door. J. C. stopped outside the door to the young gunfighter's cell.

"Let me guess, you had it all worked out in your mind how it was *supposed* to come off. You were gonna just ride into town, call me out, and face me in a gunfight in the dusty street.

"After you *outdrew* me and killed me, you'd have the reputation as the man that killed J. C. Holderfield, the *fastest gun in Texas* in a *fair* gunfight. Is that about how it was *supposed* to be?"

The gunfighter didn't reply, he just stared at J. C. with pure hatred in his eyes.

"Do yourself a favor, boy," J. C. told him. "Go back to Missouri and forget this notion of being a *gunfighter.* If you had got your wish back there, you'd be dead right now and *nobody* remembers a loser."

"I can beat you!" the young gunny screamed.

"No, boy, you can't. Forget it. Tomorrow we'll put you on your horse and send you riding. If I ever set eyes on you again there won't be no *fair gunfight,* I'll shoot you on sight. Are we clear on that?"

"But—but I heard you were a *fair* man."

"I am. Otherwise you'd be dead right now."

That said, J. C. turned and walked from the office, leaving the *would be* gunfighter to ponder his words.

One day, two well-dressed Mexicans rode into town and reined up in front of the marshal's office. They tied their mounts and opened the door. J. C. and his deputy were going over some paperwork.

"Can I help you?" J. C. asked.

"Are you J. C. Holderfield?" the best dressed of the two asked.

"I am. What can I do for you?"

"I am *Fernando Garcia*; this is *Manuel Lopez*. We have come all the way from Laredo, Texas to speak with you."

"That's a far piece. What's on your mind?"

"We want to hire you."

"I've already got a job."

"We have heard of your ability to bring law and order to a town where there is none. We have a problem that only a man like you can solve. We are prepared to offer two hundred American dollars a month, plus all the fines you collect, if you will come and help us."

"That's a lot of money. You must have some mighty big troubles to make an offer like that. What seems to be the problem?"

"As you can imagine, our population is largely Hispanic. After the end of the war, when the Rio Grande was established as the boundary between Mexico and the United States, the citizens of Laredo voted to petition the United States Army authorities to cede our town back to Mexico. The petition was rejected. As a result, half of our citizens moved across the river and formed Nuevo Laredo.

"There is still much bitterness between the two communities. Mexican raiders from across the river regularly raid our town, robbing us, kidnapping our women and children, and forcing them into prostitution in Mexico.

"We are desperate, senor. Desperate times call for desperate measures. The army says it's a local problem and refuses to get involved. They have even declared

Laredo off limits to their soldiers; that is why we come to you. Will you help us?"

As J. C. listened to the men, he felt sympathy for them and their problem. During the war, the Texas Rangers occupied the town of Laredo, and he had spent some time there. He tried to imagine what it would be like if he and his family faced a similar situation and no one would help.

He sat silently for a time.

"Are you fellows staying in town for a day or two?"

"We will stay as long as we need to," the spokesman said.

"Give me time to talk with my wife about it and I'll give you my answer tomorrow."

"Gracias, senor. We will be at the hotel."

They turned and left. Del Fisher didn't say anything for a time. Finally, he looked at J. C.

"You ain't seriously considering going are you?"

"Don't know yet," J. C. told him. "Need to talk with Opal about it."

"But why, J. C.? You're set for life here in Dallas. Everybody likes you and respects the job you're doing. Why would you go to a place that has that kind of troubles like that and take a chance of getting your head blowed off?"

"Like I said, don't know yet."

The deputy slowly nodded his head and dropped the subject.

As usual, Opal had supper ready when he got home from work. As he did each day, he went to the baby's cradle and stared down at his daughter for a time. Reaching a hand, he gently touched her cheek with a finger before turning, taking Opal in his arms, and hugging her close—today, even closer than usual.

"What's wrong, J. C.?" she asked, obviously somehow sensing something.

"Just something at work," he told her. "We'll talk about it after supper."

The fried chicken and all the trimmings were even better than usual. They talked small talk during supper. Opal shared several new things Molly had done that day. After supper Opal poured them another cup of coffee and sat down.

"Tell me about it," she said.

"I had two visitors all the way from Laredo, Texas today. They offered me a job. I told them I needed to talk with you about it."

"What kind of job?"

"Same as here—except more money."

"Do you want to go?" she asked.

"No, but I feel like I have to."

"Why do you feel like you have to?"

He explained exactly what the men had told him, not leaving anything out. She listened intently, watching him as he spoke. He saw tears seep from her eyes as he told about the fate of the women and little girls.

"We have a good set-up here in Dallas," he said. "We could most likely stay on here the rest of our lives. We have a good home, a decent living, our community is growing, and things are pretty peaceful now.

"On the other hand, Laredo is a long ways away, we'd have to find a place to live, and the job would be dangerous, at least for awhile. I've got a little money put back, but not enough to last long in case something should happen to me. Laying it all out side by side, I'd be a fool to take the job."

"But there's more to it than that, ain't there?" she said.

He nodded.

"I heard someone ask a preacher one time why he came to that particular town. The preacher said, "*I'm called to show sinners the error of their ways. This is where the sinners are.*"

"When I pinned on this badge, I swore to uphold the law, to protect the innocent, and bring the guilty to justice. To me, it's not just a job; I reckon you could say it's more like a *calling*. If I decide to go to Laredo, it will be because I'm a lawman—that's who I am."

For a long minute she sat silently, staring off into space.

"J. C., you were a lawman when I married you. I would never want to change who you are. Do what you feel like you need to do. Me and Molly will go wherever you go."

CHAPTER XVI

J. C. reined the carriage to a stop on the outskirts of Laredo. It had been a long, hot ride from San Antonio where he had purchased the carriage. Beside him, Opal held their daughter in her arms. Their luggage, containing all their worldly possessions, was loaded behind the seat. Blackie followed the carriage on a lead line.

Laredo, Texas was spread out before them. A dozen or more businesses were housed in *adobe* buildings that stood in two rows and formed the single street. Other smaller, but similar buildings were scattered in clusters behind the businesses.

A sudden, strong puff of wind gusted from nowhere as if serving as their only welcome. It gathered a blinding cloud of dust and swept it along the single street that ended at the river on the far edge of town.

At first glance, the place looked like any sleepy, peaceful, completely vacant small town.

Not a single person or animal could be seen. It looked as if the town had been completely abandoned.

"There's nobody here," Opal said, with surprise and concern.

"Welcome to Laredo," he said, slanting a look and smile at Opal. "In this part of the country, everything comes to a halt in the heat of the day; it's their traditional *nap time*. They call it *siesta.*"

"I could learn to like that tradition," she said, smiling broadly. "*Gracias, senor,*" she added, doing a quick mock bow with her head.

"I'm impressed. I figure we'll both learn the language pretty quick."

"Well, you've just heard about all of it I know so far," she laughed.

He flicked the reins, and the team of horses moved briskly forward. As they drove down the street, they looked closely at the businesses.

A small blacksmith and livery was the first. Two, skinny, half-starved horses stood with their heads down inside a makeshift, mesquite-woven fence. A grey donkey beside them raised its head for a look as they drove past. An *adobe* building with broken windows and a door hanging askew sat vacant on the other side of the street. Next door was the *cantina*. The bright red letters on the wide, sickly-looking green front wall identified it as such. It was easily the largest building in town. Two wooden hitching rails in front were empty.

A wide, empty space where a burnt-out building once stood was next. Beyond that sat the large *general store,* owned by one of the men who had come to see him. He reined their carriage to a stop in front of the store.

Opal waited in the carriage while J. C. went inside. *Fernando Garcia* sat in a chair with his feet propped in another chair, sound asleep and snoring loudly. J. C. coughed loudly, hoping to wake him—it did. The storekeeper jerked wide-eyed awake, recognized J. C., and stood quickly to his feet with his hand extended.

"Ah, S*enor* Holderfield, it is so good to see you!" he said, taking J. C.'s hand with both of his and shaking it for a long moment. "We have been expecting you."

"It's a long ways from Dallas," J. C. said. "My wife and baby are outside. Could you show us to the house you said we could use?"

"Of course. My horse is tied behind the store. Let me get it and I'll show you."

J. C. went back outside to wait with Opal and Molly while the storekeeper got his horse. He came around the building riding a grey gelding.

"Follow me," the storekeeper told them, reining his mount through a wide opening toward a wooded hillside south of town. The narrow road wound up a steep hillside and ended up in front of a beautiful *hacienda* with a red tile roof. A ten foot *adobe* wall completely surrounded the large house. The walled *hacienda* sat in the midst of a grove of large, stately oak trees.

"*This* is where we're going to live?" Opal asked, wide-eyed with amazement.

"Reckon so," J. C. said, as amazed as she was.

Mr. *Garcia* quickly dismounted and opened the wide, wooden, double gate and led the way inside.

J. C. pulled their carriage through the gates and reined to a stop in front of their new home. He helped Opal and the baby to the ground. Opal still stared wide-eyed at the beautiful *hacienda.*

"This once belonged to *Alonso Monterroza* before he and his family moved across the river. He is a very wealthy man. It is now owned by Laredo. It is yours to use as long as you wish. If it is not furnished as you wish, S*enora,* we will provide whatever you need."

"*Gracias, Senor,*" Opal said. "I'm sure it will be fine."

A stone path wound through a flower garden with a stone pool in the center. Water bubbled from a fresh spring and spilled over, forming a small stream that meandered through the flower garden and exited the compound through a small, barred opening.

"The natural spring provides all the fresh water for the *hacienda,*" the storekeeper told them. "Come. I show you the inside."

A covered veranda spanned the entire front of the home. Hanging baskets with colorful, flowering bougainvilleas lined the veranda. *Senor Garcia* opened one of the heavy, double doors into the *hacienda* and escorted them into a wide hallway with doors on both sides.

"The first door on your right leads to a den, completely furnished. The door to your left is to a dining room. A doorway in the dining room leads to the kitchen. Further along the hallway are the bedrooms, three of them.

"*Jose and Maria Gonzales* are your caretakers and servants provided by our town. You will find *Maria* to be an excellent cook and housekeeper. If there is anything else you need, *Senora,* just ask."

"I don't know what to say, Mr. *Garcia,*" J. C. said. "We weren't expecting all this."

"You take care of our people, *senor,* and we will take care of you."

"I'll do my best. Do you have a jail?"

"*Si,* but I'm afraid it has been damaged. We will see that it is repaired quickly. I will tell *Jose* and *Maria* that you have arrived."

"I'll take a look at the jail as soon as we get settled in," J. C. told him.

Mr. *Garcia* left and they were alone. No sooner had he left than Opal rushed to J. C. and hugged him close, careful not to crush little Molly.

"Oh, J. C.! This is the most beautiful home I have ever seen! I just can't believe it!"

"It sure is something, ain't it?" he agreed.

"I hope we never leave!" she said excitedly. "I could live here forever!"

"Forever is a long time," he laughed.

They were still excitedly exploring the spacious house when *Jose* and *Maria* arrived. They were very gracious and seemed like a nice couple to both J. C. and Opal. After their introduction, *Maria* immediately set about preparing the supper meal.

"I'm gonna ride down and take a look at the jail," J. C. told his wife. "I'll be back in time for supper."

"Be careful," she said, hugging him close.

"Don't worry, I will."

He mounted and rode down the hill toward town. He had no trouble finding the jail. The sign over the door, as well as the front of the building, was riddled with bullet holes. He reined up, tied his horse to the small hitching rail in front, and stepped through the door.

He stopped just inside and swept the cluttered room with a slow look—it was a disaster.

The small desk was upended with every drawer out of it. The gun rack had been ripped from the wall and lay on the floor. There were two chairs; one had only two legs and the other had no bottom in it. Papers and trash were strewn around the small office.

The adjoining jail cell was separated by an *adobe* wall and thick wooden door. The jail cell itself seemed to have come through with little damage.

Sure gonna take some cleaning up, but it'll do for now, he thought.

As he left the office, he saw several townsfolk starting to move about. A young Mexican boy passed by leading a skinny burrow with a load of river reeds tied to its back. The boy stared at him as he passed. He nodded *howdy* to the boy. He knew from his previous time in Laredo they often used chopped-up river reeds as reinforcement in making *adobe* bricks.

Another younger boy herded a dozen goats down the street, undoubtedly taking them to the river to drink. A woman across the street was hanging strings of red peppers in front of her small business.

Laredo was coming to life.

He toed a stirrup and swung into his saddle, reining Blackie toward the river. He reined up on the north bank and sat his saddle.

The Rio Grande River was no more than a hundred yards wide this time of year at the Laredo-*Nuevo Laredo* crossing. A mounted rider would get wet to his knees, but would have no trouble riding across, and therein lay the problem. It was a simple matter for riders to cross the river, do their evil, and flee back to Mexico where Texas law officers had no authority.

It was like the age-old children's game of *tag*. A player was free to do what he wanted, but when pursued, rushed back to *home base* where he couldn't be *tagged*.

It was a real problem all along the American-Mexican border and frustrated all American law enforcement officers.

It all boils down to this, he decided. *I've got to catch the bad guys before they have a chance to get back across the river.*

He remembered the two signs he had made up while still in Dallas and decided to wait until the next day to put them up.

There was lots of activity along the street of Laredo now. Children were running and playing with dogs chasing after them, barking at their heels. Across the river, he saw a loaded freight wagon headed toward the river crossing, most likely headed for Laredo or maybe points beyond. Older children were playing near the water's edge, and one older Mexican sat on the bank fishing—it was a peaceful scene.

He unwound his leg from around the saddle horn and reined Blackie back toward his new home.

Jose was tending the flowers when J. C. rode through the gates of the *hacienda* and dismounted. The Mexican caretaker hurried to take charge of J. C.'s horse.

"There ez a small barn behind the *hacienda, Senor.* I will brush, feed, and water your mount before I put him in the stall."

J. C. was pleased that the caretaker could speak English, which would sure help in the communication department.

"*Gracias, Jose.*"

The caretaker led the horse away. J. C. headed for the house. His timing was perfect. Supper was already on the table. Opal was sitting at one end allowing Molly to nurse. The large, oblong, mahogany dining table had three chairs on each side and one at each end.

The table was set with china plates and silverware. In the center was a beautiful arrangement of fresh flowers surrounded by steaming platters of Mexican-style food.

"Looks mighty fancy," he told Opal.

"*Maria* is a wonderful cook," Opal said. "It will be nice to eat someone else's cooking for a change."

"I'm sure gonna have to do them a good job to pay for all this."

"You will," she told him, looking up from the baby and flashing him a big smile.

Opal was right; *Maria* was a good cook. He couldn't remember ever enjoying Mexican food as well.

After supper they retired to the den. *Maria* brought coffee and cups and served them.

"We will leave now," she told them. "I have three grandchildren to prepare supper for."

"Where are their parents?" Opal asked.

A sad look crossed *Maria's* face at the question.

"Our daughter was taken by the evil *Luis Ramos.* They killed our son-in-law when he fought them. The children were too small for their use."

"How long ago was this?" J. C. asked.

"Three months. We still pray that she is alive and will someday return to us."

J. C. felt frustration, knowing that after that long it was unlikely she would ever return. He resolved right then and there to stop this sort of thing.

Opal rose and hugged *Maria.* The bereaved mother swiped the tears from her eyes and hurried out of the room.

"What sort of men would do something like that?" Opal asked bitterly.

"The sort of men we are dealing with," J. C. told her.

When they were ready to retire, they discovered a hot bath prepared and waiting and the sheets on their bed already turned down.

"Can you believe all this?" Opal asked, again surprised with it all. "I could get spoiled to this way of life really easy."

She put little Molly to bed and hurried to the bath tub.

"I'll be there shortly. I'm gonna have a hot bath before I come to bed."

"Take your time," he told her.

Later, they lay quietly in one another's arms. Three large candles flickered on a brass stand, lighting the large bedroom with a soft glow. For a time nothing was said. J. C. stared up at the ceiling, enjoying the almost reverent closeness.

"Do you remember back in Dallas when you said you felt your job was similar to the *calling* by God of a preacher?"

He nodded.

"Well, maybe it is. Maybe you are God's guardian angel for these people."

"Right now I feel more like an *avenging angel.* After hearing how they took *Maria's* daughter and killed those children's father, I can't wait to lay eyes on this *Luis Ramos* character."

"I love you, J. C.," she whispered, cuddling even closer and kissing him softly on the neck.

"I love you, too," he said.

CHAPTER XVII

True to his word, *Fernando Garcia* and a crew of a half-dozen men were at the jail when J. C. arrived just after sun-up. Some were carrying out the broken desk and chairs and replacing them with new ones. Others were sweeping the hard-packed, dirt floor. One fellow was patching the bullet holes in the front wall, while yet another was painting the front with dark brown paint.

"How do you say *good morning* in your language?" J. C. asked.

"¡Buenos dias," Mr. *Garcia* told him.

"¡Buenos dias," J. C. repeated. "I'll learn."

"Learning the Mexican language is easier than learning the English language," the storekeeper told him.

"Wouldn't seem so."

"Your language has many words that are spoken the same, but mean something very different."

"I have enough trouble with English, let alone Mexican. Looks like your people are doing a good job."

"We are very glad you are here, *senor.*"

"When do these bad guys usually show up?"

"Usually at night, although lately they have come during the day several times."

J. C. nodded.

"I brought two signs with me," he said, holding up one of them for the storekeeper's inspection.

Garcia read the sign and nodded.

"That will be hard to enforce, I'm afraid," he said.

"At first it will, but after awhile they'll get the message. Tell me about this *Luis Ramos* fellow."

"He is a very bad man! He leads a band of the worst kind of men ever born. All of them are killers, rapists, and robbers."

"How many men does he have?"

"Sometimes a few, usually many. They shoot down anybody that resists them."

"Is he the *real* leader or does someone else give the orders?"

"I do not know the answer to your question, *senor.*"

"It's okay, I'll find out. Are there others besides *Luis Ramos?*"

"*Si,* but none as bad as he is."

A day passed without incident—then two. His signs warning visitors against carrying firearms in town were installed at the bank of the river before entering Laredo, as well as the other edge of town.

His office and jail were finished and he had visited every business in town, meeting all the owners, and offering his assistance in case they needed help.

He had taken to returning to his office after supper with Opal, figuring it would be nighttime when they came—he was right.

The pounding sound of many horses reached his hearing. Since there was little or no movement after dark in Laredo, he knew immediately the source of the sound. He rose quickly, took his black, flat-brimmed hat from the wall peg and set it in place. He took down his Tennessee long rifle from the wall rack and stepped through the open door of his office.

A three-quarter moon was the only light in the street except the light that spilled through the open door of the *cantina* up the street.

A wad of riders had emerged from the river and was galloping up the street. He quickly judged their number to be near a dozen. The lead rider carried the sign that J. C. had nailed to a tree near the river bank.

J. C. raked back the striker of his rifle and stepped to his left so as not to be framed in the light from his office. When they drew near, the riders reined down to a slow walk.

They spread out and lined up stirrup-to-stirrup facing his office. He assumed the one carrying his sign was *Luis Ramos.*

He was a big man, heavy around the middle and wide-shouldered. He wore a mustache and his hat hung down his back, held in place by a leather thong. Twin belts criss-crossed at his waist and held two holsters with pearl-handled pistols.

"I am Luis Ramos!" the man announced loudly in pretty good English, as he slammed the sign to the ground in front of J. C. "What is meaning of this?"

"Can you read English as well as you speak it?"

"You make a joke, eh?"

"It's no joke. From now on, it's against the law to carry firearms in Laredo."

Every man laughed loudly, including the leader, ridiculing both the law and the lawman. J. C. stood motionless with his rifle cradled in the crook of his arm and his gaze fixed upon the leader.

"Who are you to make such a law?" the leader demanded.

J. C. knew it was show time. He knew they were only a few words from a confrontation, and he wanted to act before they did. In one smooth movement he swung his rifle to his shoulder, pointed directly at the leader's wide chest.

His swift, aggressive action caught the leader by surprise. He saw the man's eyes go wide, but he also saw the leader's followers grab for their pistols.

"If even one of your men pulls iron, I'll blow you out of your saddle!" J. C. shouted loudly.

"*¡Espera!*" the leader shouted to his men. "Do as he says! He will kill me!"

From the corner of his eye, J. C. saw the men ease their hands away from their guns.

"I'm J. C. Holderfield. I'm the new town marshal in Laredo. Tell your men to ease their guns out *real* careful and drop them on the ground. One wrong move by anyone and you're a dead man!—DO IT!"

"*Déjà tu armas!*" the leader told his men angrily. One by one the followers reluctantly did what their leader told them to do. When the last man had dropped his pistol into the street, J. C. focused his unwavering gaze on *Luis Ramos*.

"Now you!" he told the leader through clenched teeth. "Either drop your guns or use them, whichever suits you."

For a long moment the leader hesitated, undoubtedly weighing his chances of drawing his sidearm and firing before J. C. could simply pull the trigger.

"I won't say it again," J. C. said calmly, but with a sound of finality.

Obviously, the bandit leader came to the conclusion that there was no way he could win this standoff. He slowly, carefully, removed his pistols using only his thumbs and a single finger, and dropped them to the ground.

"Good decision," J. C. told him. "Now, have your men dismount one at a time, take three steps forward, and kneel on the ground with their hands on their heads." The leader gave the order. J. C. watched as one by one they did as he had said. It took a few minutes, but finally they were all kneeling with their hands on their heads, and the leader was still sitting in his saddle.

"I've got a nice, clean jail cell right inside. One at a time, tell them to go in and make themselves at home inside the cell. One wrong move, just one, by any of them and I'll kill you!"

Once again, he watched as the bandits did as he ordered. When the last one was inside, he looked again at *Luis Ramos.*

"Now it's your turn. Climb down and let's go join your men."

Luis Ramos swung a leg over his saddle and stepped to the ground.

"I will cut your heart out and stuff it in your mouth for this, *gringo!*" The bandit leader spat the words from his snarling mouth.

When the bandit leader joined his men in the small jail cell, it was packed—they were jammed together shoulder-to-shoulder. J. C. closed the barred cell door and locked it.

"You fellows make yourselves at home; get used to it, you may be there awhile."

He left and closed the heavy, wooden door between the jail cell and his office. He put his long rifle in the gun rack on the wall and then walked outside. He gathered up all the weapons and piled them in a corner of his office. He bunched the twelve horses, tying some to the hitching rail and the rest to each other. He returned to his office and hung his hat on the wall peg, shucked his coat, hanging it on the back of his chair. He sat down behind his desk and propped his feet on top of it—and waited. It took less than half-an-hour before *Fernando Garcia, Manuel Lopez,* and several more men from Laredo ventured cautiously into his office.

"What is happening?" the storekeeper asked. "We heard the bandits' horses from our homes, and now they are tied out front. Where are the bandits?"

"They're back yonder in jail where they belong."

"But how?" the town leader asked, looking confused. "How did you manage to capture them?"

"I reckon you men cleaned up the jail so good they wanted to try it out."

"You joke."

"Well, yeah, a little. Reckon somebody could take their horses up to the livery stable? *Luis Ramos* and his men won't be needing them for awhile—maybe never."

"What do you intend to do with them?"

"I mean to hang one each day until they decide to tell me what happened to the women and girls they kidnapped and who's behind all this. I just don't believe this *Ramos* fellow is smart enough to run an operation like this."

The townsmen were shocked. They exchanged guarded looks with one another.

"But can you do that, *senor*?" *Garcia* asked.

"I can unless you fellows tell me I can't, but if you do, I leave the next day. It all boils down to this. Do you want a peaceful town or do you want these murderers to keep stealing your women and girls and murdering your people?

"As I recall, back in Dallas you told me *drastic times call for drastic measures*. It's up to you; I either do this my way or I don't do it at all."

Mr. *Garcia* looked around at the others and then nodded his head.

"Do what you have to do. We will support you."

"Good! That's what I was hoping you would decide. Right now I need a few things. First off, reckon somebody could find me a pot of coffee? I'll be here the rest of the night. I'd be much obliged if somebody could take word to my wife and let her know I'm alright. Tell her I'll be home in time for breakfast.

"I'm gonna need a small cot so I can sleep here in the office at night for awhile. Reckon three or four of you fellows could act as my deputies until this is over? There's plenty of guns right over there in the corner. I'll need some help guarding the prisoners.

"Last of all, I'm gonna need a dozen stout ropes."

"I will take care of it myself, *senor,*" *Fernando Garcia* said.

After they brought him a pot of coffee, two of the townsmen stayed to help guard the prisoners. J. C. looked in on his prisoners from time to time. There wasn't enough room in the small cell for them to all lie down at once. Obviously, they figured out how to take turns; some

lay on the floor while others stood, and then they
changed—but it must have been an uncomfortable night.

Daylight finally came and with it came another visit
from *Fernando Garcia* and another young Mexican
named *Philippi Rodriquez.*

"We have decided to hire *Philippi* as a full-time
deputy, if that's alright with you?"

J. C. looked the young fellow over with a quick look.
He was clean-cut, young, and had a good look about him.
J. C. stuck out his hand.

"Good to have you," he told the young fellow. "Can I
trust you?"

"*Si, senor.* I will do whatever you tell me to do."

"Fair enough," J. C. said, shaking the young man's
hand and handing him a badge from a desk drawer. "Pick
out one of them gun rigs from the corner that suits you."
Leaving his new, young deputy in charge, J. C. mounted
and rode up the hill to their *hacienda.* Opal was up and
allowing little Molly to nurse.

"I was so worried about you, J. C.," she told him.
"Thanks for sending me word what was going on. I
understand you captured *Luis Ramos* and his whole
gang."

"Yeah, I reckon you could say I got lucky."

"Did you find out anything about what happened to
Maria's daughter?"

"No, not yet, but I'm working on it. I'm gonna try to
get some answers in the next few days."

Maria brought him a cup of coffee and some
breakfast. He wolfed it down hurriedly.

"Can't you take time to rest some before you go
back?" Opal asked.

"Not really. I got a lot of work to do. They're bringing in a cot to put in the office; I'll try to get some rest there."

After he finished his breakfast, he walked over and stared down at their daughter for a minute. He hugged Opal and kissed her before hurrying back to his horse. He found twelve coiled ropes stacked on top of his desk, clearly visible through the door of the jail cell. He then walked into the jail area, leaving the heavy, wooden door wide open. He took his new deputy along to interpret what he had to say.

"Did you fellows sleep well?" he asked cheerfully.

Philippi relayed his words.

His question was met with a string of loud cursing. He waited until it died down a bit.

"Here's what's gonna happen. I'm gonna ask some questions. See them ropes out there? If I don't like the answers, I'm gonna hang one of you each day until I learn what I want to know."

He waited for his deputy to relay what he said.

"First question . . . What happened to a young wife and mother you kidnapped about two months ago named *Carlotta Morales?*"

He waited a long minute for a reply to his question. Nobody said a word. He shrugged and pulled his big Colt Dragoon. Behind him, his new deputy did the same. J. C. thumbed back the hammer and unlocked the door to the cell. He pointed a finger at one of the men.

"You! Step out of the cell."

The man's eyes rounded and he refused to exit the cell.

"Either step out of the cell or I'll shoot one of the others until you do. I'll count to three before I start shooting. One . . ."

The man didn't move.

"Two . . ."

Suddenly the other gang members shoved the man J. C. had chosen from the cell. He slammed the cell door shut and locked it. He shoved the prisoner through the heavy, wooden door and left it open on purpose. He cut a small length of rope and tied the man's hands behind him. He then selected one of the ropes from his desk and marched the man from the office into the street.

A giant oak tree with wide-reaching limbs stood at the edge of town toward the river. Townspeople emerged from buildings and followed along behind as J. C. and the deputy marched the condemned gang member to the oak tree.

He tied a slip knot and looped it around the man's ankles. He threw the loose end of the rope over a sturdy limb and, with the deputy's help, hoisted the man off the ground. When his head was dangling four feet from the ground, he tied the loose end around the trunk of the tree.

A crowd of onlookers stood in hushed silence as the condemned screamed for help, pleaded, and cursed the mother who gave birth to the lawman. The crowd watched for awhile and then, one by one, went on about their business, leaving the gang member to his own fate.

J. C. and his young deputy stood and watched for several minutes.

"How long will it take?" the deputy asked.

"Couple of days, more or less," J. C. told him.

"Reckon we'll find out when he does."

It became a morning ritual. Each morning J. C. asked the same question, with the same results, and each morning they selected one of the gang and carried out the same routine.

As the days passed, the crowd of townspeople there to witness the upside-down hanging of one of the gang members grew larger.

On the third day the angry townspeople began filing past and spitting on the hated gang members who were hanging upside-down: some lashed them with river cane. J. C. and his deputy found the first man dead on the fourth morning.

Day after day the hangings continued. Somehow, word reached *Nuevo Laredo* and several made the journey across the river to witness the daily executions. A few were critical of what was happening, but most were aware of the atrocities that had been carried out against the citizens of Laredo and were in agreement of the punishment being administered.

On the seventh day, a United States Army officer from nearby Fort McIntosh (formerly called Fort Crawford) rode into town and reined up in front of the marshal's office. J. C. was sitting at his desk when the officer entered.

Out of old habit, J. C. immediately stood to attention before he caught himself and stuck out his hand in greeting.

"I'm J. C. Holderfield, Colonel. I'm the town marshal of Laredo.

"Good afternoon, Marshal. I'm Col. Walter Russell, commandant of Fort McIntosh."

"Have a seat, Col. Russell. What can I do for you?"
"I've heard your name somewhere, Mr. Holderfield, but I can't seem to place where."

"I served in the Texas Rangers during the war under General Zachary Taylor. I was part of his personal security detachment. I also was stationed here in Laredo for a time."

"Yes, of course, that's where it was. So you've returned to Laredo in a different capacity?"

"Yes, I reckon so."

"Well, back to the reason for my visit. The United States Army is concerned about these *hangings* you're conducting. We are working to improve relations with our neighboring country of Mexico, and all these hangings are causing considerable problems. We've received a dispatch from the Mexican government, lodging an official protest. Simply put, these executions must be stopped immediately."

As J. C. listened to the *dressing down* from the colonel, he felt heat rising up through his neck. He could feel the flush spreading across his face.

"Now hold on right there, Colonel. It's my understanding the leaders of Laredo went to the army pleading for help to stop the robberies, killings, and the kidnapping of their women and girls who are then taken across the river into Mexico and sold into prostitution. Is that not true?"

"Well, yes, I seem to remember having that discussion with several of them."

"And they were told, obviously by *you,* that it was a *local problem and the army couldn't get involved!* Isn't that also true?"

"But all these hangings change the circumstances. The United States Army simply cannot permit Mexican citizens to be summarily hanged without benefit of even a trial! They have rights, too!"

"What about the *rights* of three small children left orphan because that scum right back there in my jail shot down their father and kidnapped their mother and hauled her across the river to be sold into prostitution? What about *their rights,* Colonel?

"Where was all this *concern* when these murdering gangs rode across the river right under your nose and terrorized the citizens of Laredo? Where were you then? Now, when they finally get their can full of it and do something about it, all of a sudden the *circumstances* have changed just because some paid-off Mexican official lodges a complaint!

"Maybe I *misunderstood,* Colonel, but I thought your job was to protect the citizens of *this* country, not Mexico. Isn't that the purpose of the fort?"

"Well, yes, that's *part* of our mission."

"Then I strongly *suggest* you either do your job or stay out of the way and let me do mine. Frankly, Colonel, I've been fighting the urge to contact some of my friends in Washington about the matter, but I've held off out of respect for the army. Now I'm beginning to have my doubts."

"I—I don't think that will be necessary, Marshal Holderfield. I'll handle the matter with Mexico. Good day to you, sir," he said, standing, clamping his hat in place, and hurrying from the office.

The following morning the hangings proceeded and continued until the only prisoner left in the cell was *Luis Ramos.*

On the morning of the twelfth day, when J. C. and his deputy went to the jail cell, they found a shaking and broken man cowering in the far corner of the small cell.

"Get on your feet, *Ramos,*" J. C. told him. "It's your turn."

"I will tell you what you want to know, *senor,*" he said in a quivering voice. "*Por Favor,* do not hang me like the others!"

"You got my word. I won't hang you like the others if you tell me what I want to know. Who is your boss?" J. C. asked.

"*Alonzo Monterroza!* It was him, not me. He is the one you want!"

"Where is *Carlotta Morales*? What happened to her?"

"She is a servant in the home of *Alonzo Monterroza.*"

"And the others; what happened to all the others you and your men took?"

"They were turned over to S*enor Monterroza.* As God is my witness, I do not know what happened to them after that."

"Alright, I believe you. Step out of the cell."

Luis Ramos climbed to his feet and stumbled from the cell. J. C. held his gun on him while Deputy *Rodriquez* tied his hands behind his back. Together, they led him from the jail into the street. When they turned toward what had become widely known as *the hanging tree, Ramos* suddenly balked and twisted a look at the marshal.

"Where are you taking me? You're not going to hang me! You gave your word!"

"I gave my word I wouldn't hang you like the *others*, and I won't. I hung them by their feet; we're gonna hang you by your filthy neck until you're dead."

The entire citizenry of Laredo was there to witness the hanging of the hated murderer. They watched in complete silence as J. C. placed the rope around the neck of the bandit leader. But as J. C. and his deputy hoisted *Luis Ramos* into the air, the onlookers suddenly broke into a loud cheer—finally—justice was done.

CHAPTER XVIII

It was a simple matter to learn where the richest and most famous citizen of *Nuevo Laredo* lived. The old freight driver who travelled regularly between the two towns proudly told J. C. about the sprawling *hacienda* on the hill overlooking *Nuevo Laredo* where *Alonzo Monterroza* lived.

Crossing the river into Mexico where he had no jurisdiction, getting into the *hacienda* that likely would be heavily guarded—rescuing *Carlotta Morales,* and bringing *Alonzo Monterroza* back to Texas might be a little more difficult. He knew if he got caught he was a dead man, no question about it.

Alonzo Monterroza has lived a double life. He has posed as an upstanding citizen while his hired gangs murdered innocent citizens of Laredo and kidnapped young women and girls so they could be sold into slavery as prostitutes, making him a rich man.

He's got to be stopped. Wrong is wrong. It is what it is.

He bided his time, waiting. A week passed—and then two.

Thunder clouds began to build in the south early. By mid-afternoon the sky was black. Thunder rumbled like rolling cannon fire. Jagged spears of lightning stabbed the ground.

By five o'clock it was as dark as midnight.

Tonight's the night, he decided.

He rode up to their home at suppertime. Opal was surprised to see him; he was earlier than usual.

"I think I'll stay at the office tonight," he explained, not wanting to worry Opal about what his real plans were. "I'll see how much longer before supper will be ready," she said, handing little Molly to him.

She left the room to talk with *Maria.* J. C. looked down into the bright, blue eyes of his small daughter. The baby stared up at him. He gently touched her cheek with a finger. At his touch, a smile curled her lips.

I love you, Molly. You are part of me. You and your mother are the most important part of my life. If this goes wrong tonight and I don't come back, I'll die with you and your mother on my mind and in my heart.

Two large tears seeped from his eyes and dropped upon baby Molly's face. Bending his face, he kissed them away.

"What's wrong, honey?" Opal asked anxiously as she re-entered the room. "Why are you crying?"

The emotion was so full in his throat words wouldn't come. He simply slowly shook his head.

Opal went to him, wrapped her arms around his neck, and hugged him close. He looked up at her through tear-stained eyes.

"I love you, Opal. I didn't know it at first, but I've always loved you. You've given me the greatest gifts a woman could give—your love and my daughter."

It was a terrible night for man or beast. No rational person would be out on a night like this. A howling wind captured the driving rain and drove it into J. C. as he tied three horses in a thick grove of cedar bushes just in sight of the sprawling *hacienda.*

It sat on the very top of a steep hill overlooking *Nueva Laredo.*

Reckon Alonzo Monterroza's got a thing about living on top of a hill overlooking town, he thought.

He unconsciously touched his Colt Dragoon and the wide-bladed throwing knife he had carried on his belt since he was a young boy just leaving home.

Only the vague, dark outline of the walled *hacienda* was visible through the driving rain and pitch blackness of the night.

Bending low, he shielded his face with an arm from the stinging raindrops as he hurried toward the wall. Coiled over his other arm was a long rope with a grappling hook tied securely to one end.

He reached the wall forty yards or so left of the double front gate. Squinting his eyes, he looked up. The solid *adobe* wall was ten feet high with broken glass embedded in the top. With a hand, he felt along the wall as he made his way to a corner. Once around the corner, he hurried another thirty yards before deciding this was as good a place as any.

Holding the coiled rope in his left hand, he grasped the rope several feet from the hook. He swung the hook upward over the top of the wall, hoping the thunder and wind would muffle the sound of the metal hook against the wall.

He tugged on the rope. The hook caught. He tested it with the strength of his arms—it held. Placing a booted foot against the wall and using the strength of his arms, he walked himself up the wall to the top.

His gloves absorbed the sharp edges of the broken glass embedded in the top of the wall, and he pulled himself over and dropped to the ground on the inside of the compound.

Several lanterns hanging from metal posts were scattered around the large yard inside the compound walls. With the driving rain, their light was shrouded into only small circles immediately around the post.

Pausing and listening intently, he searched the darkness for any sign that his entrance had been overheard or observed—he detected no threat.

Moving bent over, he made his way through a wide, flowering garden to a covered veranda that completely circled the large *hacienda.* Pressing his back against the front of the house, he moved cautiously along the wall. A guard with a rifle across his knees sat in a chair just ahead. The guard's chin was slumped against his chest—obviously asleep.

J. C. tip-toed forward, slipping his wide-blade knife from its leather sheath. With his knife in his right hand, he moved silently until he was behind the guard. Reaching out, he clamped his left hand over the guard's mouth and pressed the razor-edge of the knife against his throat.

Leaning over, he whispered into the guard's ear. *"Carlotta Morales, ¿donde esta?"*

The guard hesitated for only a moment before pointing down the veranda to a door. Removing his knife from the guard's neck, he replaced it in his leather sheath, removed his heavy Colt Dragoon from its holster and struck the guard on the back of the head. He slumped over, unconscious.

Using one of several leather thongs from his pocket, he quickly tied the guard's hands behind him. Cutting a sleeve from the guard's shirt, he stuffed it in the man's mouth and tied it with another leather thong.

He picked up the guard's rifle and flung it as far out into the courtyard as he could. He hurried down the veranda to the door the guard had indicated. He pushed on it quietly—it opened—he stepped silently into the room.

The room was black dark. He couldn't see his hand in front of his face. He stood motionless and held his breath. The faint sound of someone's even breathing reached him—he crept toward the sound.

The sound came from someone lying on a floor pallet. Again following the sound, he clamped his hand over the sleeper's mouth. The sleeper came instantly awake. J. C.'s hand muffled the cry from a woman's voice.

"Carlotta Morales," J. C. whispered, bending low over her. *"Maria Gonzales* sent me. Do you understand?"

The woman relaxed and nodded her head.

"I'm going to remove my hand from your mouth. Don't make a sound, understand?"

Again the woman nodded.

He carefully removed his hand from her mouth.

"Can you light a candle?" he asked.

She rose from the pallet and moved. In a moment a small candle was lit.

The woman was dressed in a white gown that came to her ankles. She quickly slipped a white housecoat over it.

"I've come to take you home," he told her, watching her face. Her eyes widened and tears wet them.

"Are there other guards besides the one out on the veranda?" he asked.

She nodded and raised two fingers and pointed outside. He nodded understanding.

"Are there any in the house?"

She shook her head.

"Alonzo Monterroza; where is he?"

She pointed to a door opposite the one where he had entered.

"Take me to him," he told her.

A frightened look swept over her face.

"It's alright. Just show me where he sleeps."

She took up the small, metal candle stand and opened the door she had indicated. It led to a wide hallway. She slipped quietly down the hallway. J. C. followed with his gun in his hand.

She stopped in front of a tall door and pointed. He nodded and took the candle from her hand. Quietly, he pushed open the door. Light from his candle filled the large room with a dim glow.

Two people lay in a large bed with a white canopy over it. It looked like one was a large man and the other a young girl. J. C. crept toward the bed with the candle in one hand and his gun in the other. *Carlotta Morales* followed.

When he stood beside the bed looking down at the snoring man, he felt an overwhelming urge to just shoot him while he still slept—but that was too easy. He handed the candle back to *Carlotta,* clamped a cupped hand over the sleeper's mouth, and pressed the nose of his Colt Dragoon hard against the man's forehead.

Alonzo Monterroza woke with a start. His eyes rounded in surprise and shock.

"Does he speak English?" he asked over his shoulder.

"Yes," *Carlotta* replied.

"See to the girl if she wakes up," J. C. told her quietly. "Who is she?"

"Her name is *Ana Ramirez* from Laredo. She is but a child, only twelve years old."

"That scum bag!" J. C. said through clenched teeth. "Are there others like her still here?"

"No, she is the only one."

"Light another candle. Then get the girl up and take her to your room. I'll be along shortly."

J. C. flipped the heavy man over onto his stomach and tied his hands behind his back. He cut a piece from a bed sheet and stuffed it into the Mexican's mouth, tying it in place with another leather thong.

Carlotta and the girl were gone. The Mexican was sweating badly. Great drops of sweat popped out from his forehead and ran down his face.

J. C. replaced his gun in its holster and withdrew the big knife. He put the sharp point into the edge of the man's nose and leaned close.

"Where are the others?" he asked quietly.

The man shook his head as if he didn't know.

J. C. flicked the knife upward, slicing open one of the man's nostrils. Blood spurted upward and fell onto the Mexican's face.

J. C. moved the knife into the other nostril.

"Where are the others?" he asked again.

The terrified man mumbled but couldn't talk for the gag.

"I'm gonna remove the gag, but if you try to cry out, I'll cut your throat! Understood?"

The terrified Mexican nodded his head. J. C. removed the gag.

"Where are the others?"

"The little one is the only one. The others are gone."

"Where?"

"They are sold to government officials in *Monterrey*. From there, I do not know."

J. C. paused and thought about what the man said. He shook his head in disgust and helplessness.

What more can I do? he thought. *It would be impossible to track them down.*

"You are one sorry piece of trash!" He spat the words into the Mexican's face. He wanted to cut the man's throat, but what good would that do? Then, a thought hit him.

"Where's the money?"

The Mexican's eyes widened even more. J. C. knew he had struck a nerve.

"The money you got from selling those women and girls! Where is it?"

The Mexican slave trafficker shook his head violently.

J. C. grabbed an ear and with a quick slice, completely severed it from his head and clamped a hand over his mouth to stifle the scream.

Blood gushed from the hole left by the severed ear.

"Where's the money?" J. C. repeated.

The man pointed with his head. J. C. grabbed him and pulled him to his feet. The rich Mexican stumbled to a mahogany cabinet against the wall and again nodded with his head.

J. C. swung open the two doors that covered the top half of the cabinet. Several large drawers were behind the doors. He jerked one of them open. It was filled with stacks of American money, all separated and held with wrappers.

A second drawer was filled with large-domination Mexican currency. There were four drawers in all. Two held American money; the other two were filled with Mexican money.

Suddenly, the door to the bedroom was slammed open. Two guards rushed in with rifles leveled. J. C. reached an arm and wrapped it around the Mexican's neck, pulling him between the guards and himself. Before they could react, they fired.

The two slugs tore into the fat Mexican, killing him instantly. J. C. grabbed his Colt Dragoon from its holster, thumbed back the hammer, and shot both guards twice each. They both crumpled to the floor.

Carlotta and the girl appeared at the door with concern showing on their faces. They relaxed when they saw that he was alright and the others were all dead.

"Is there anyone else in the house?" J. C. asked quickly.

"No," *Carlotta* answered.

"Then find me a pillow case or tow sack and let's gather up this money. I think the nice folks of Laredo deserve it."

CHAPTER XIX

After the rescue of *Carlotta Morales* and the return of *Ana Ramirez to her folks,* J. C.'s reputation spread far and wide.

The townsfolk of Laredo put the money he turned over to them to good use. They built a new town square, a church and school, and hired *Philippi Rodriquez* as full-time deputy.

A steady stream of bad men fleeing to Mexico passed through Laredo, but due to J. C.'s reputation, most of them either shucked their guns upon entering town, or just kept on riding across the river.

Mostly, things were quiet and peaceful in Laredo. Women and children felt safe to walk down the street, even at night. A tense, but tolerable, relationship continued with Col. Russell and the army at Fort McIntosh.

Months passed and turned into a year—and then two.

They celebrated Molly's third birthday on July 12, 1854—it was a happy occasion.

On a particularly hot day in August of that year, three riders rode into Laredo just before sundown. J. C. was in his office getting ready to ride home for supper when his deputy rushed into the office.

"Three riders just rode in," he said. "You might want to come and have a look."

J. C. pushed up from his chair, shrugged into his long-tailed, black coat and took his hat down from the wall peg.

He followed *Philippi* outside.

The three riders rode abreast. Each wore a canvas, long-tailed duster and walked their mounts slowly down the street. When they reached the *Four Aces Saloon*, they reined up at the hitching rail. Before dismounting, they sat their horses and slowly searched both directions of the street.

They stepped slowly to the ground and tied their horses to the rail. J. C. noticed that two of them stood aside, waiting until the tallest fellow stepped up onto the boardwalk before they followed—it was obvious the tall fellow was the leader. He wore a wide mustache that was pointed on the ends and a black, flat-brimmed hat identical to J. C.'s.

J. C. stared at the tall one until the man pushed casually through the bat-wing doors of the saloon. Something about the way this one moved—the way he walked with a confidence few men conveyed was worrisome.

"Got me a bad feeling about this bunch," J. C. told his deputy. "Take the shotgun this time and go in through the back door. I'll take the front. Be careful."

Philippi took the shotgun from the gun rack on the wall and broke it open; he thumbed in a shell and closed the gun.

"Let's go welcome them to town," J. C. said, lifting his Colt Dragoon and settling it back into the holster gently.

His deputy hurried around the saloon. Once he turned the back corner, J. C. stepped through the bat-wings.

The three strangers all stood at the bar sipping fresh drinks. Two of the men flicked a quick look when the marshal stepped inside. J. C. noticed that the tall man never even glanced his way. J. C. casually stepped a few steps inside the door and stopped.

"You fellows just passing through?" he asked.

His question drew a long look from the tall fellow.

"Who's asking?"

"I'm J. C. Holderfield, town marshal here in Laredo."

"Heard of you," the tall fellow said.

J. C. saw his deputy slip silently through the back door and move sideways, shotgun in hand.

"I reckon you didn't see the sign at the edge of town. We don't allow firearms in town limits."

J. C.'s words brought a thin, mocking smile from the tall one.

"Tell me, *Marshal*, who's gonna take our guns? You?"

"Yep. One way or the other."

"What does that mean—*one way or the other?*"

"Well, the easy way would be for you to turn them over now and get on with your drinks—no problem."

"And if we don't?"

"Mister, you don't wanna know about the hard way."

"That sounds to me like a threat, *Marshal*."

"No, just telling you how it is, that's all."

"That's mighty big talk, seeing how there's three of us and just one of you."

"Might want to count again. My deputy's standing right yonder behind you with a scattergun pointed at your backs, and he's got a mighty itchy trigger finger."

The tall man never bothered to look, but his two companions did and moved their hands away from their side arms.

"Step aside, boys," the tall one told his companions. "This here's between just me and this marshal. I rode all this way to kill him, might as well get on with it."

As he spoke, he squared around to face J. C. straight on and brushed the edge of his canvas duster back behind the butt of his Colt Dragoon, identical to J. C.'s. His two companions moved away, out of the line of fire.

"Now why would you want to kill me?"

"To prove to myself and the world I can."

"Too bad," J. C. said casually.

"What's too b..."

He never got to finish his question. Without warning, J. C.'s hand darted to his pistol, drew it, and fired in one lightning-swift motion. Once—twice—three times the big Colt Dragoon blasted.

The tall fellow was caught totally by surprise and never got his gun out of its holster. His eyes walled in shock. His face contorted. The impact of the .44 slugs slammed him backwards. His booted feet staggered in a dance of death. And then his legs buckled under him. He crumpled over with three holes in his chest, all within the span of a hand.

"That you won't get to finish your drink," J. C. answered the man's half-question, but the tall gunman never lived to hear the answer.

He turned to the man's two companions, still holding his smoking gun.

"Pick him up, throw him across his horse, and get him out of town."

"You didn't give him a chance!" one of the men protested.

"I gave him a chance—he didn't take it. A man tells me he's gonna kill me, I take him at his word. By the way, what was his name?"

"Frank Monday, from Missouri."

The next several years were *golden years* for J. C. and his family. Being the town marshal of Laredo, Texas became nothing more than a dawn to dark job; nothing more serious than Saturday night fights, an occasional family dispute, or a rare robbery happened.

Molly was growing, becoming a beautiful young girl, and excelling in the new school in town. Opal was enjoying being a wife and mother and living in their large *hacienda* complete with servants—life was good.

Then, J. C. noticed that Opal wasn't feeling well. She seemed to not be her normal, energetic self. She felt bad most of the time—something was wrong. But every time he asked her about it, she laughed and passed it off as if it was nothing serious.

She usually never complained about anything, but she told him that her stomach had been hurting lately. Then one day he walked in on her and found her vomiting. He rushed to get a wet rag to bathe her face and noticed she had vomited up blood.

He decided right then and there that he was going to take her to San Antonio to the doctor. He asked the town council for a leave of absence and explained why.

"Take whatever time you need, J. C.," the council told him.

"I'll be back if I can, but my wife's health is my highest priority right now. If it's something serious, I doubt I'll be back."

The following day, J. C., Opal, and Molly left on the early morning stage for San Antonio. It was a long, hard trip and they arrived four days later. Opal had been sick most of the trip.

Doctor Henry Williams was a young doctor in San Antonio and had quickly earned the reputation as the best in town.

J. C. and Molly waited impatiently in the waiting room of the hospital while Opal was being examined. When the doctor emerged, J. C. didn't like the look on his face.

"Could I talk with you alone?" he asked.

J. C. asked Molly to wait down the hall. She protested, but finally agreed.

"What's wrong with my wife, Doctor?"

"I'm afraid your wife has a tumor in her stomach. That is the source of the bleeding. I'm unable to determine how long she has had it, but judging by the size of it, I suspect she has had it for some time.

"As far as I can determine, I'd guess it's about the size of a large apple, but I'm afraid it will undoubtedly continue to enlarge."

"What can be done about it?"

"I wish I could tell you it can be handled. Unfortunately, that's just not the case. Medical science hasn't advanced to that point yet. At some point in the future, I'm sure we will discover new methods to deal with these things, but right now there simply isn't much we can do. I can give her drugs that will relieve the pain for awhile; beyond that, I'm sorry."

J. C. felt as if his world had just come crashing down. He was devastated.

"How—how long does she have?"

"It's impossible to predict; a few months, not much more."

"When can I see her?"

"Give the nurse a few minutes and then you can go in."

The doctor stood and shook hands with J. C.

"I'm sorry, Mr. Holderfield. I wish I could give you more hope."

J. C. nodded understanding. The doctor turned and hurried away.

For a time he stood there in total shock. He wanted to turn and run—to get away—so he could loose the flood of tears that was straining for release. He wanted to—but he couldn't—he had to think about Molly, and Opal—he had to be strong.

"What did the doctor say, Daddy? Is Mother going to be okay?"

He looked down into the questioning eyes of his daughter—his precious daughter.

What can I say? How can I tell her? Should I tell her?

"Let me go in and see your mother alone for a few minutes and then we'll talk, okay?"

"But Daddy, I want to see her, too. Why can't I go in with you?"

"I need to talk with her alone for a few minutes. Please, Molly, wait here for me. I'll be back in just a few minutes and I'll explain everything."

J. C. paused just outside the door to Opal's room. He closed his eyes and took a deep breath and pushed the door open.

Opal lay on an iron bedstead with pressed, white sheets pulled up to her neck. She had on a clean, white gown. Her eyes were closed.

He approached her bed quietly and stood looking down at her. She was so very beautiful!

Her eyes suddenly opened and her gaze found his.

Can she tell by my face that it's serious? What should I say? Should I try to act cheerful?

Should I tell her everything's gonna be alright, even if it isn't?

He leaned down and kissed her on the cheek. She never took her eyes off of his.

"It's bad, isn't it?" she asked, her lips quivering.

He nodded.

"As bad as it gets?"

Again he nodded.

A hand suddenly escaped from underneath the sheet and covered her mouth, but it failed to muffle the cry that erupted from deep inside her. Reaching his arms, he pulled her to a sitting position and hugged her to him. He held her until her sobbing subsided, kissing away her tears and swiping away his own with the back of his hand.

"Tell me exactly what the doctor said," she pleaded. "Don't hold back anything."

How can I do that? he thought. *How can I tell her she has only a few months to live?*

But he decided if their situation was reversed, he would want to know.

He told her.

As he spoke, she kept her unflinching gaze fixed on his eyes. When he finished, she closed her eyes and slowly nodded.

"What do we tell Molly?" he asked.

"The truth," she said. "I've never lied to her. I won't start now."

"Want me to tell her?" he asked.

"No, I will. Go get her and let me talk with her alone."

He nodded and left the room. He found Molly in the waiting room staring out the window.

"Your mother wants to see you," he said simply.

She nodded and went to Opal's room. J. C. took Molly's place at the window. He stared out into nothingness for a long time.

While Molly was inside with Opal, J. C. thought a long time about their situation.

Things have quieted down in Laredo, but being a lawman is still a dangerous job. What if that last fellow had killed me? With this situation with Opal, what would happen to my wife and daughter? If I wasn't around, what would happen to our daughter after . . . , he couldn't bear to think of losing Opal.

The mere thought of losing his wife stabbed at his heart, and then there was the added question of what would happen to Molly if he got himself killed and then his wife passed? The only answer was one he couldn't accept and made his heart hurt even more.

I've got to make some changes, he decided then and there. *I'll go somewhere where nobody knows me. I've got a little money put back; I'll buy us a little farm, settle down, and take care of my wife for whatever time we have left together. Then I'll raise my daughter.*

CHAPTER XX

"Where we going, Daddy?" Molly asked, as they climbed into the stagecoach.

"We'll know when we get there," J. C. told her, taking a seat beside Opal. Molly sat in the seat across from them.

"Is it a long ways?" Molly persisted.

"Most likely."

Opal smiled at her husband and watched as the stagecoach rolled up the street, leaving San Antonio behind.

"How long will it take to get there, Daddy?"

"It'll take awhile, but we're gonna take our time and enjoy the trip."

That seemed to satisfy the inquisitive nine-year-old.

The road between San Antonio and Austin was well-traveled. They made good time and arrived by nine o'clock that night. They checked into the Austin Hotel. Opal was tired and ready for bed, but Molly was beside herself with excitement.

"This is the first time I ever stayed in a real hotel!" she said excitedly, looking through the window at all the folks on the street, even as late as it was.

"We'll stay here a couple of days and rest up before we move on," J. C. told them.

That made Molly even happier.

"Can we walk around town tomorrow, Daddy?" she asked.

"Yep."

Two days later they left Austin on their way to Waco. It took them two days to travel the next leg of their journey. They had to lay over one night in a way station. The old couple who ran the station made over Molly and they all enjoyed the stop-over.

Waco was exciting because of the ice-cold spring they visited and the wide Brazos River. They spent only one night in Waco and left the next day for Tyler, Texas, but had to lay over one night in a small town called Corsicana, Texas.

It took them a full day to go from Tyler to Shreveport, Louisiana. They passed through Marshall, Texas on the way. Opal had a sick spell and they spent three days in Shreveport. Molly got to see her first steamboat while they were there.

Since there was no stage service from Shreveport to Arkansas, J. C. bought a covered wagon and two teams of horses. He learned that once they reached Little Rock, Arkansas, they could catch a stagecoach that would take them to their destination, Fort Smith, Arkansas. He figured he could sell the wagon and teams once they reached Little Rock.

Five days after reaching Shreveport, they set out on their journey in the wagon.

"This reminds me of our trip when we first went to Texas," Opal said, as they rode along.

"Yeah, that seems like a lifetime ago," he agreed.

"Tell me about it," Molly said.

Opal spent the next hour relating every detail she could remember about that adventure. Molly listened with undivided attention.

"That must have been exciting!" she said.

"As I remember it," Opal told her, "it was more scary than exciting, not knowing if we would be scalped around the next bend in the road."

"It got pretty hairy there a time or two," J. C. agreed.

"Why did you pick Fort Smith, Arkansas for us to go to?" Opal asked.

"A friend of mine I rode with in the Texas Rangers is a Deputy United States Marshal there. I figured he might know where I might find what I'm looking for."

"What are you looking for?" she asked.

"I'd like to find a marshal's job in some small town where nobody ever heard of me; one where we could settle down and live in peace without having to look over my shoulder."

"That would be nice. I worry about you," she told him.

"I know."

They took their time and enjoyed the trip. They stopped early each afternoon and found a good camping place, cooked supper, and sat around the campfire together. Opal had two bad periods of sickness, but always seemed to recover quickly.

Three weeks after leaving Shreveport, they arrived in Little Rock, Arkansas. J. C. sold the wagon and teams for a profit and made arrangements for seats on the next stage to Fort Smith.

Three days later they arrived in the bustling city of Fort Smith, Arkansas. They were amazed. It was a beehive of activity with folks hustling about. The stage driver unloaded their luggage and a carriage took them to the Ward Hotel.

"After we get checked into our room, I'll go look up my friend and be back before dark," J. C. told them. "Might be best if you stay in the hotel until I get back."

He asked the desk clerk where he could find the Deputy United States Marshal's office.

"That would be up the street and on your left. His office is in the fort."

J. C. thanked him and walked out onto the busy street. He passed three saloons just in the first block.

Must be a rough town, he thought.

He found the fort overlooking the Arkansas River. He climbed the wooden stairs and made his way along the wood-floored hallway. He came to a door that identified it as the marshal's office and stepped inside.

Two men were in the office; one of them was his friend from his Texas Rangers days. Herb Dean glanced up as J. C. walked in, and then did a double-take. He quickly stood up and stuck out a welcoming hand.

"J. C. Holderfield!" he said. "What in the world are you doing here?"

"Came to see an old friend," J. C. told him, shaking Herb's hand.

"Last time I heard about you, you were town marshal in Laredo, Texas."

"Yep, but my wife's got some health problems so I decided to make a change."

"J. C., I want you to meet my boss, Chip Reece, the United States Marshal. Chip, this is J. C. Holderfield, known all over as the toughest town tamer west of the Mississippi."

The marshal rose from his chair and shook J. C.'s hand.

"I've heard of you, Mr. Holderfield. It's a pleasure to meet you."

"Sorry to hear about you wife, J. C.," Herb said.

"Anything serious?"

"As serious as it gets. Doctor says she ain't got long."

"That's too bad."

"You said you was lookin' to make a change," the U. S. Marshal said. "What kind of change?"

"Hoping I could find a quiet, little town where I could settle down and take care of my family; someplace where nobody ever heard of me."

"You could go to work for me," the marshal said. "I could sure use a man like you."

"I'm much obliged for the offer, Marshal, but from what I seen on the way over here, I'd be right back in a job like I just walked away from. I want to spend whatever time my wife has left with her and my daughter."

"What about that town marshal job down in Waldron?" Herb asked the marshal. "That sounds like what he's looking for."

The marshal nodded his head in agreement.

"Yeah, that might be just what he's talking about."

"Where's Waldron?" J. C. asked.

"It's about a half-day's ride south of here; small farming community, not much going on. Nice folks, the way I hear it."

"Sounds interesting," J. C. said. "I'll ride down and talk with them."

"If you change your mind about going to work for me, the offer still stands," Marshal Reece told him.

"I'm obliged, Marshal."

J. C. decided to leave Opal and Molly in the hotel and ride down and talk to the folks in Waldron by himself before having them make another day's ride that might be for nothing. He rented a horse from the livery and left early the following morning.

He headed south like Herb told him. After awhile, he climbed a thin road over a mountain Herb had called *Backbone Mountain.*

After having spent several years in barren, sandy country, the rolling hills and heavily timbered country looked good. It was mid-afternoon when he rode into Waldron and reined up at a blacksmith-livery. A big fellow was shoeing a team of heavy plow horses.

"Howdy," J. C. greeted.

The hostler nodded a greeting since he had several horseshoe nails between his bearded lips.

"Looking for whoever's head of the town council," J. C. said.

The hostler set the horse's hoof down and removed the nails from his mouth.

"That'd be Sam Jamison. He runs the mercantile store right up the street yonder."

"Much obliged," J. C. said, reining his mount around. He reined up in front of the store and stepped to the ground. He looped the reins around the hitching rail and stepped up on the wide boardwalk. The twin doors of the store were propped open. He walked inside.

The storekeeper looked up from behind the counter when J. C. walked in.

"Afternoon, stranger," the storekeeper greeted. "How can I help you?"

"Are you Sam Jamison?"

"Sure am. What can I do for you?"

"I'm J. C. Holderfield. I was told in Fort Smith your town might be looking for a town marshal?"

"Maybe; you ever been a lawman?"

"Yes, sir, served two years with the Texas Rangers and another three years as town marshal of Dallas, Texas. For the last six years, I've been town marshal of Laredo, Texas."

"Why'd you leave your last job?"

"My wife's sick and I've got a nine-year-old daughter. I'm looking for a quiet, little place to settle down and take care of my wife without having to look over my shoulder all the time."

"You ain't a wanted man, are you?"

"No, sir. The United States Marshal and his deputy in Fort Smith can vouch for me, if need be."

"We're a small town, Mr. Holderfield. We can't pay much. The job pays fifty dollars a week. It's yours if you want it."

"I'll take it. Do you know of a house for rent or for sale close by?"

"Matter of fact, there is. The old Sutton place is for sale; nice place, too. I think the bank's got it. Talk to Mr. Wilkerson over at the bank."

"I'll do it. I'll do you folks a good job. You got my word on it."

"I believe that, Mr. Holderfield," he said, sticking out his hand for a handshake to seal the agreement.

From the mercantile store he went directly to the bank and walked in.

"I'd like to see Mr. Wilkerson," he told the lady behind the teller counter.

"I'm Grady Wilkerson," a well-dressed fellow said from a desk behind a railing. "How can I help you?"

They shook hands.

"I'm J. C. Holderfield. I just hired on as the new town marshal. I'll be moving to Waldron with my wife and nine-year-old daughter. Mr. Jamison said he thought there was a house available nearby. Could you tell me about it?"

"Of course. Welcome to Waldron, Mr. Holderfield. I think you and your family will like our little town. Yes, the Sutton place is for sale. Roy and Melba both passed on and our bank ended up with the property.

"It's a nice home and is just two blocks from the town marshal's office. It has two bedrooms and sits on a large lot. I'd be glad to show it to you."

"You're a busy man. If it's alright, I'll just walk up and take a look around. What are you asking for it?"

"Well, since you're going to be our town marshal, we could let you have it for twelve hundred dollars. We could even set it up so you could make yearly payments, if you like?"

"Let me take a look at it first and then we'll talk," J. C. said.

"Of course. It's the white house with green trim. It has a white picket fence around it. You can't miss it."

They shook hands again and J. C. left the bank. He headed up the street to look at the house. On the way, he passed a building with a sign that identified it as the *TOWN MARSHAL'S OFFICE & JAIL.*

He decided to look at the house first and then look at his office. He spotted the house while he was still a block away. From the street, it looked beautiful. He opened the gate of the picket fence and climbed the steps to a wide front porch. A porch swing hung from the ceiling on two chains. He paused and gave the swing a gentle push with a hand.

The inside proved to be as impressive as the outside. He explored every room and had made up his mind even before he finished the tour—it would make them a good home.

He decided right then and there to buy it.

He headed back to the bank and in less than half-hour's time they owned the home outright. He paid for it from the money he had saved from his job in Laredo. From the bank, he went to look at his office and the jail. He found it to be a *typical* town marshal's office and jail, no different from a dozen others he had seen scattered across Texas.

He went to the livery and rented a large freight wagon and a team of horses, tied his rented horse behind it, and headed north to Fort Smith. He meant to ask Opal to pick out furniture for their new home before they left Fort Smith, since he didn't see any at Jamison's store in Waldron.

Opal enjoyed getting to choose their new furniture. Each time, she would stop and ask if they could afford whatever piece of furniture she was looking at. J. C. always laughed and assured her that they could afford it.

The big freight wagon was loaded down when they left Fort Smith. It was an exciting time for their whole family.

By mid-afternoon they pulled up the street of Waldron. Townsfolk came out of stores to greet them and followed them up the street to their new home. The men helped unload the furniture while the ladies helped place it in its proper location. Several ladies brought vittles, and when the work was finished, they all enjoyed a welcome meal together. By the time the evening was over, it was like they were already old friends. Molly met and made new friends her own age.

Life was good for the Holderfield family in Waldron, Arkansas.

CHAPTER XXI

The next six months were the best months of J. C.'s entire life. The job of town marshal was the easiest job he ever had and allowed him plenty of free time. He got to spend more time with both Opal and Molly and they grew closer than ever before.

Then one day as he was sitting in his office browsing through a Fort Smith newspaper, Molly burst breathless into his office.

"Daddy! You got to come quick—it's Mother!"

J. C. shot up from his chair and grabbed his hat on the way to the front door. As hard as he tried to stay up, he couldn't begin to keep pace with his ten-year-old daughter. She beat him in the house and was kneeling beside Opal when J. C. rushed into the bedroom. Opal lay on the floor where she had fallen. A large puddle of vomit mixed with blood was all around her.

"Go get Doctor Monroe," J. C. told his daughter. "Hurry!"

He hurried to the kitchen and returned with a pan of water and a towel. He bathed her face and wiped it from her hair. He picked her up and laid her gently on the nearby bed. He felt her pulse—it was weak—so weak he could barely feel it.

He was kneeling beside the bed holding her hand when Molly and the doctor rushed in.

"I can't hardly feel her pulse," J. C. told the old Waldron country doctor.

The doctor didn't reply, but took a stethoscope from a small, black bag. He placed the ear pieces in his ears and placed the round, flat portion against Opal's chest. He listened intently for several minutes, moving the flat part to her side and back.

He placed the flat of his hand against her stomach and pressed slightly. Opal lay with her eyes closed, unconscious. Her breathing was slow and shallow. The old doctor removed the stethoscope from his ears and hung it around his neck. The look on his face sent cold chills racing through J. C.'s whole body. The doctor looked at J. C. and then at Molly.

"Molly," the doctor said quietly. "Would you go get Mrs. Jamison? We need her."

Molly looked at the doctor for a long moment and then at her father. Her face suddenly contorted. Tears breached her eyes as she turned and ran from the room.

"I didn't reckon she needed to hear what I gotta say," the old doctor explained. "I'm plumb sorry, Marshal, but ain't no other way to say it 'ceptin straight out; your wife's dying. I reckon you need to be saying your *goodbyes.*"

A wrenching pain in the depth of his stomach gave birth to a great sob that raced upward to his throat and threatened to erupt—he swallowed it back down—this wasn't the time for weeping—that would come later. Right now he needed to be strong for Opal and Molly's sake. He struggled to control his emotions.

The doctor moved to a nearby chair with his black bag in his lap. Molly returned with a distraught Mrs. Jamison. She stood at the foot of Opal's bed for a few moments, staring at her new friend and dabbing at her tear-wet eyes with a handkerchief, before whispering comforting words to both Molly and J. C. and slipping quietly from the room.

Molly knelt beside J. C. and circled an arm around her father's waist. She was sobbing heavily, leaning her head against his shoulder. He circled his daughter's shoulders with his free arm and pulled her close.

Suddenly. . . miraculously . . . Opal's eyes opened and looked directly at J. C and Molly. A slight, weak nod of her head toward her daughter was all Molly needed to lean forward and hug her mother close. For several long moments, they hugged.

Reaching a weak hand, Opal pulled her daughter up to look deep into her eyes.

"I love you, my darling Molly. Be brave. Take care of your father for me."

Molly burst into tears, jumped up, and ran from the room.

After Molly left, Opal directed her look at her husband.

Her lips moved weakly in a soft whisper.

"Hold me. . . I want you to hold me until I go."

J. C. bit his bottom lip, choked back a sob, and lifted her to a sitting position. He wrapped his arms around her and hugged her close. His silent tears dripped onto her shoulder.

"I love you with all my heart, Opal."

"I love . . . you," she whispered weakly before drawing a long, deep breath—they were her last words.

THE END

Author's Note:
You can read the "rest of the story" of J. C. Holderfield in my Award-winning book, Manhunter, voted the "Best Western Novel" of 2002.